"I'm here to care for my sister's babies.

"I already love them. I did from the moment I learned they were coming."

"I can take care of them. I want you to leave," he said.

"Nathan, be reasonable. You need help."

He faced Maisie with his arms crossed over his chest. The moon came out from behind the clouds, bathing his face in its cold light. "It can't be you."

"Why not?"

"Because every time I look at you, I see Annie. I don't want you here."

The bitterness in his clipped words left Maisie speechless. He walked away into the darkness.

"But they're all I have left of her," she whispered as a deep ache filled her chest. "Please don't make me leave them."

She felt Charlie lick her fingers. He whined as if he knew she had been hurt by Nathan's words. She dropped down to hold the big dog close and draw some comfort against the new grief she felt.

How could she change Nathan's mind?

After thirty-five years as a nurse, **Patricia Davids** hung up her stethoscope to become a full-time writer. She enjoys spending her free time visiting her grandchildren, doing some long-overdue yard work and traveling to research her story locations. She resides in Wichita, Kansas. Pat always enjoys hearing from her readers. You can visit her online at patriciadavids.com.

Books by Patricia Davids

Love Inspired

North Country Amish

An Amish Wife for Christmas
Shelter from the Storm
The Amish Teacher's Dilemma
A Haven for Christmas
Someone to Trust
An Amish Mother for His Twins

The Amish Bachelors

An Amish Harvest
An Amish Noel
His Amish Teacher
Their Pretend Amish Courtship
Amish Christmas Twins
An Unexpected Amish Romance
His New Amish Family

Visit the Author Profile page at Harlequin.com for more titles.

An Amish Mother for His Twins

Patricia Davids

LOVE INSPIRED
INSPIRATIONAL ROMANCE

LOVE INSPIRED®
INSPIRATIONAL ROMANCE

Recycling programs for this product may not exist in your area.

ISBN-13: 978-1-335-56706-2

An Amish Mother for His Twins

Copyright © 2021 by Patricia MacDonald

This edition published by arrangement with Harlequin Books S.A.

For questions and comments about the quality of this book, please contact us at CustomerService@Harlequin.com.

Love Inspired
22 Adelaide St. West, 40th Floor
Toronto, Ontario M5H 4E3, Canada
www.Harlequin.com

Printed in U.S.A.

He healeth the broken in heart,
and bindeth up their wounds.
—*Psalm* 147:3

This book is dedicated to the wonderful staff of Chapman Valley Manor who have cared for my father, Clarence, during these trying times. My heart is full of gratitude. Thank you.

Chapter One

His head was ready to explode.

Nathan Weaver sat at the kitchen table in his one-room cabin with his hands pressed to his throbbing temples. He had come to Maine to live a quiet life and to forget. For six months he'd done just that. In less than a week his peace was gone. He'd never know solitude again.

Both babies were crying at the top of their lungs in their Moses baskets near his feet. His hound, Buddy, howled in accompaniment. The yellow cat, yowling to be let out, had crawled to the top of his screen door and hung splayed like a pelt on the wall. The kettle's piercing whistle was close to drowning out everything. He closed his eyes and moved his hands to cover his ears. It didn't help.

Buddy stopped howling and started barking

a challenge. The abrupt change made Nathan look up. An Amish woman stood outside the screen door. For a moment his heart froze. It wasn't possible.

"Annie?" he croaked.

Was he hallucinating? It couldn't be her. Annie had died in childbirth six days ago.

The woman opened the screen door. His cat launched himself into the night, just missing her head. "Not Annie, Nathan. It's Maisie Schrock."

He blinked hard. Maisie? Annie's twin sister? She was a widow who lived in Missouri caring for their ailing father. What was she doing in Maine?

She gazed inside, an expression of shock on her face. She held a suitcase in her hand. Buddy stopped barking and went to greet her with his tail wagging. The babies continued to cry.

"Annie died." Nathan swallowed against the pain. Saying the words aloud still didn't make it feel real.

"I know. The hospital told me yesterday. I'm so sorry. My sister is with *Gott* now," Maisie said with a catch in her voice. There were tears in her eyes.

Seeing her grief propelled Nathan to his feet. He stepped to the stove and pulled the kettle off the fire. The whistling died away, but the babies kept crying.

"What are you doing here? If you've come for the funeral, it's over." Maisie lived in the tiny Amish settlement near Seymour, Missouri, where he had married her sister last fall.

"I was afraid of that. I'm sorry I wasn't here to share your burden." She focused her attention on the babies. "Boys or girls?"

"One of each."

"Are they hungry?" She crossed the room to kneel beside their Moses baskets. Gifts to Nathan from the hospital staff when they'd learned he didn't have a place for the babies to sleep. Maisie lifted a child to her shoulder and the baby quieted. Buddy, the stray hound that had shown up a few weeks after Nathan arrived in Maine, followed her with his tail wagging.

Nathan raked his hands through his hair. "I don't know what's wrong with them. I tried feeding them, but they wouldn't take much and then they started crying as soon as I put them down."

She stroked the baby's cheek and rocked her gently. "Aw, *liebling*, it's okay."

Liebling. Darling. He used to call Annie that. Before she left him with only a cryptic note a bare two months after their wedding. He still didn't understand why. He took some comfort in knowing she was trying to get back to him before she died. He would have forgiven her and taken her back, but would he have been able to trust her? Or grow to love her again?

Maisie laid her cheek against the baby's fine auburn hair. "*Ach*, you look like your mother. Your poor *mamm*. How you must miss her."

Maisie straightened and wiped her cheeks again. "I think they just want to be held."

She wrapped the blanket snugly around the baby and handed her to Nathan. He took his daughter gingerly, afraid he might somehow damage her with his big coarse hands. Maisie picked up his son, and he quieted in her arms.

Suddenly there was silence in the cabin. The pounding in Nathan's head eased. "What are you doing here? I only wrote to you yesterday. I think it was yesterday. How did you find me?"

Maisie moved to the beat-up blue sofa he'd claimed from the side of the road where someone had dumped it. The two broken legs had been replaced with rocks. His brown-and-black hound parked himself at her feet.

"Annie sent me the money to come three weeks ago, along with your address. She said she was on her way here to make amends with you. In her letter she said she wanted her babies to grow up in an Amish family, with their father. She regretted leaving you, Nathan."

"Three weeks ago? If she knew where I was why didn't she write or call?"

While he didn't own a cell phone or have a landline in his home, like most Amish he shared a community telephone with neighbors. It was housed in a small building centrally located between the homes. The phone shack contained an answering machine, so his boss and others could leave messages.

Maisie shook her head. "I don't know why she didn't call you."

"I found out five days ago that I was a widower and the father of twins all in one breath when the bishop came with the news that Annie had died in childbirth. Eight months without a word from her. That doesn't feel like she regretted it."

"Leaving you as she did was a terrible thing. I know that, but you must find forgiveness in your heart."

"Must I? Sure, I forgive her." It was easy enough to say the words, but he didn't mean them. Not yet. Maisie knew it, too. He saw it in her expression.

Her eyes softened. "She was coming home to have your babies. She asked me to come and stay for a month or so to help her and you. Of course, I said yes. She knew twins would be lots of work."

"They are."

"But you haven't found anyone to help you."

It was a statement more than a question. He hung his head. He didn't want to depend on anyone. He'd never joined the Amish congregation in New Covenant so he didn't expect help from them. "I can raise them by myself." But could he?

"You don't have to, Nathan. I'm here now. We can get through our loss together."

His wasn't the only grief he had to consider. Maisie had lost a beloved sister. Her twin. The blow must have been devastating, but she was offering to help him, a man her sister couldn't bear to stay married to.

Did Maisie wonder what he had done to drive Annie away from her family and her faith? Did she blame him, as others had? After trying to push these questions out of his mind for months, he suddenly wanted answers.

"Did you know Annie had planned to leave me?"

Maisie glanced at the child she held. "Can we talk about this later? I'm tired and I think they need to be fed."

She looked so much like Annie. She was a painful reminder of the woman he'd loved and lost…twice. A woman who had betrayed her wedding vows and destroyed the love he'd once had for her.

When Annie left him she'd done more than break his heart. She'd taken away his dreams of a family. There was no divorce allowed in his Amish faith. He would have remained married but alone, until his death. That was why he had retreated to the wilds of Maine six months ago. He was used to being alone. He'd been alone his whole life until he'd met Annie.

Nathan belatedly recalled his duty as a host. He couldn't send Maisie away tonight. Unless her driver was waiting outside. "How did you get here?"

"I came on the bus. I was walking this way when a kindly woman stopped and offered me a ride in her car. She said she was a neighbor of yours, Lilly Arnett."

Lilly had a home about three miles down the road. She wasn't Amish but she was a good neighbor. She'd gone out of her way to bring Maisie up to his remote cabin. "Is she still outside?"

"*Nee*. She said she had to get back to do chores. Do you have bottles and formula for them?"

"The hospital sent some supplies when they dismissed the *kinder*. Formula, bottles, diapers, a couple of blankets that the nurse said she wasn't supposed to give away, but she couldn't see sending me home without a way to keep them warm."

"Clearly a woman with a good heart. I'll fix some formula if you will hold…what is his name?" She looked at him.

Nathan hadn't decided yet, for either babe. Annie should have told him what she wanted to call them. Annie should be here taking care of them. Maisie had the same flame-red hair, the same bright green eyes, and freckles across her nose. She even had the same dimples in her cheeks when she smiled. It was painful to see her and know she wasn't the woman he'd married.

He changed the subject. "Would you like some tea or hot chocolate? The water on the stove is hot. There's some bread and blueberry jam in the cupboard."

"I'll fix it. Do you want something?" She got up and settled his son in his free arm.

"Nee." He wasn't hungry.

She crossed her arms and gazed at him with her eyes full of sympathy. "When was the last time you ate?"

"I don't remember."

"Then you should at least have some toast." She went into the corner of the cabin that held a wood-burning cookstove, two cupboards, a sink and an icebox. She located the bread, then put it in the oven to toast. Next, she fixed hot cocoa for herself and opened two small bottles of premade formula the hospital had sent home with Nathan. She had a few bites of toast and a sip of the cocoa, then took the baby from Nathan and sat down to feed him.

Nathan's daughter made short work of her bottle. He glanced over to watch Maisie cooing at his son. Why couldn't it be Annie holding her own baby? Why did it have to be Maisie, who looked like Annie in every way? It was heartbreaking to see her and know she wasn't their mother.

"Don't forget to burp her," Maisie said.

He had forgotten. He took the bottle away from his daughter and shifted her gingerly to his shoulder. She burped twice and then began bobbing her head, looking for more to eat. He settled her in the crook of his arm and let her finish. When the bottle was drained, he looked at Maisie. "Should I burp her again?"

"Ja." She had his son cradled in her arms, gazing at his face, then she put him in his basket. To Nathan's amazement, the baby went straight to sleep.

Maisie turned to Nathan. "I'll put her down if she is finished."

"I think she is." He handed the babe to her and sat back, rubbing his hands on his thighs. Maisie was good with the babies. He wasn't. It was hard to imagine he was now the father of two. Nothing had prepared him for this, but he would manage. He had always managed alone.

He'd built this cabin with his own two hands. He would find a way to raise his children. Annie had at least given him back the dream of having a family. He would be grateful for that when he wasn't so exhausted.

Maisie took his daughter and laid her down. She fussed for a moment but then quieted and went to sleep.

Maisie covered a yawn. Nathan nodded toward the small loft at the far end of the cabin. "There's a bed and extra blankets up there. You're welcome to them."

Maisie scanned the rest of the one-room cabin. "Where will you sleep? I don't want to put you out of your own bed."

"I have a cot in a room down in the barn. I'll sleep there. The barn was here when I bought the place. I slept in it until the cabin was finished. It's comfortable." He didn't like being in the same room with her. She was a distressing reminder of what he'd lost.

"All right. Would you like to talk now?"

Talk about Annie and her death? He suddenly realized he wasn't ready for that. "Tomorrow."

He got up and left the cabin.

Maisie watched Nathan walk out of the house with tired, stumbling steps. She had no idea what to make of him. Like everyone in her community, she wondered what had driven Annie to leave her new husband. Why had her sister stayed away from her family and the people who loved her? From Maisie, the person who knew her best in the whole world?

The answers to those questions may have died with Annie, but Maisie wasn't ready to give up. Nathan had to have some idea of what went wrong in their marriage. Maisie needed to know the truth from him now that she couldn't learn it from Annie.

After making sure there was enough formula to see the babies through the night, she walked outside. She was tired from the long trip but too wound up to sleep. Her grief was too new and sharp.

She had boarded the bus in Springfield, Missouri, filled with joy and hope for the first time in almost a year. She was going to be reunited with her beloved sister, to meet her sister's babies and help take care of them. She was going to learn the reason why Annie had left Nathan and disappeared, something Annie said she couldn't tell Maisie over the phone but had promised to reveal when they were face-to-face again. She had no way of knowing her sister was already with God. Ten hours later, when Maisie changed buses outside of Philadelphia, she had enough time during the layover to call Annie and see if she had delivered her babies yet. Instead, a social worker at a hospital in Portland, Maine, told her that Annie was dead.

Maisie still couldn't absorb the fact that she would never see her sister again. Never hear her voice, never laugh at the same things or finish each other's sentences. It was if she had been cleaved in two and half of her was gone.

The loneliness and sorrow of those remaining horrible hours on the bus had been almost too much to bear. Only her faith and the thought of holding her sister's babies got her through the ordeal. Now she was here in Maine at last. Her life had purpose again. Nathan and the babies needed her.

The warm night air was thick with the scents of wood smoke and pine trees, and the sound of droning insects. The sky was overcast, with the drifting clouds hiding the moon and blocking out the light from the stars. When her eyes adjusted to the dark, she could just make out the outline of the barn and corral fence across the way. Two horses stood at the fence. She saw a shadow move beside them and knew Nathan hadn't gone to bed. She walked toward him, wondering what she was going to say. Buddy followed at her heels.

The awkwardness of the situation had her on edge. She wanted...no, she needed to help care for her sister's babies. They were her last and only connection to Annie. Holding Annie's child in her arms tonight had eased the hurt Maisie carried in her heart. Only, Nathan didn't want her here. How could she make him see it was best for all of them if she stayed?

He didn't seem surprised when she walked up beside him. Her head was level with his shoulder. She felt small beside him. One of the horses reached over the fence to nudge her arm. She rubbed his forehead. "Who is this?"

"Mack."

"And the other one?"

"Donald."

She chuckled. "You're joking."

"I didn't name them. That's what they were called when I bought them." His dry tone said he didn't find it funny.

"Someone had a good sense of humor," she finished lamely.

"I asked you a question earlier."

He was angry and bitter. She couldn't blame him. She had been angry at Annie, too. She still had a hard time believing her sister had done such a terrible thing. Now Annie was gone before she could explain. Maisie sighed deeply. "I didn't know my sister had plans to leave you."

"Do you know why she left?"

"I don't." It was the truth. All Maisie had was a vague suspicion—that Annie had left to be with another man. Telling Nathan would only heap more pain on a man who was already hurting, and maybe plant a seed of doubt that the children weren't his. Maisie couldn't do that to him. Like her, the children were all he had left of his love for Annie.

"How did she know to send you here?" he asked.

"She left a message with her cell-phone number on the answering machine at the phone shack of our bishop. You had told him you were moving to New Covenant. You had given him the name of the man you planned to work for so he could contact you in case Annie came back to our community. He told me and I called her."

"What did she say? Did she explain herself? Did she know the harm she caused? I couldn't even stay in Seymour."

"She said she would explain everything when she saw me in person. I'm sorry some people in Seymour were unfair to you."

"Unfair?" The single word was almost a snarl. "They thought I killed my wife. They sent the sheriff to search my property with dogs. They didn't believe the note she left had been written by her."

Maisie flinched away from his anger. "None of the Amish community thought that, Nathan. We were all shocked to learn of her disappearance, especially me and *Daed*. It was only some of Annie's *Englisch* friends who suspected foul play." The Porters, the influential family both she and Annie had once worked for. Wealthy people who didn't understand Amish ways even though they hired them. Maisie had married and stopped working in their home, but Annie stayed another four years, until the oldest son and his children moved away after his wife's death. Then Annie abruptly married Nathan.

"The Porters were the same people who stopped buying the lumber I cut. They stopped others from buying from me or hiring me to clear land. I couldn't make a living."

"Edward Porter and his wife loved Annie like a daughter. She was more than a nanny to their grandchildren. She took care of their daughter-in-law while she was dying."

"And I loved Annie like a wife!" he shouted.

Maisie stayed silent. Finally, he drew a deep breath. "You said the hospital told you that she had passed away. How?"

"As I said, I had Annie's cell-phone number. We exchanged a few phone calls while I was preparing to travel here. She wouldn't talk about the past, only about how she hoped to make up for the pain she had caused everyone. She was excited about having twins. She wanted daughters. She said they would be as close as she and I had been." Only they hadn't been close enough.

"Did she have names picked out?" His voice broke and he bowed his head. It was too dark to see his face, but she knew he was crying.

Maisie laid a hand on his arm, fighting back her own tears. "She wanted you to name them. I know you loved her, Nathan. I know you love her children. You will give them the life she wanted for them. *Gott* will show you the way. Trust Him. Draw strength from His love."

Nathan straightened and pulled away from her hand. "*Gott* hasn't done much for me lately. Go on with your story."

There was an edge to his voice now. Was he angry with God, as well as Annie? Maisie couldn't have made it through the last two days without God's comfort and the thought of holding Annie's babies.

Nathan needed God. He would come to see that when his grief wasn't so sharp.

"I hadn't talked to my sister for over a week so I called Annie from a bus stop in Pennsylvania yesterday to let her know I was on my way. A woman who said she worked at the hospital in Portland answered the phone. She told me Annie had…died of complications following childbirth, but the babies were fine and with you. Apparently Annie was able to tell them how to contact your bishop and have him deliver a message."

Nathan sighed heavily. "She must have been the same woman who tried to give me the phone along with Annie's things when I picked up the babies. I had no use for a phone. I told her to keep it. She said she would hold on to it for a while in case anyone tried to contact Annie then she would donate it to a charity. I didn't care what she did with it."

"I'm grateful she answered even though the news she delivered was heartbreaking."

"If I'd known you were coming, I could have delayed the burial."

"I would like to visit her grave soon. To say my goodbyes."

"I'll take you tomorrow. Then I'll take you into town and get you a bus ticket home."

Startled, she shook her head. "*Nee*, I'm here to care for my sister's babies. I already love them. I did from the moment I learned they were coming."

"I can take care of them. I want you to leave."

"Nathan, be reasonable. You need help."

He faced her with his arms crossed over his chest. The moon came out from behind the clouds, bathing his face in its cold light. "It can't be you."

"Why not?"

"Because every time I look at you… I see Annie. I don't want you here."

The bitterness in his clipped words left Maisie speechless. He walked away into the darkness.

"But they're all I have left of her," she whispered as a deep ache filled her chest. "Please don't make me leave them."

She felt Buddy lick her fingers. He whined as if he knew she had been hurt by Nathan's words. She dropped down to hold the big dog close and draw some comfort against the yawning hole of new grief she saw opening before her. How could she change Nathan's mind?

Chapter Two

The impatient whinny of a horse pulled Nathan out of a sound sleep. The call was repeated by a second horse, then a third. He opened his eyes and stared at the bare wooden timbers over his head. Why was he in the barn?

He sat up and rubbed his face. Memories of the past week came flooding back and hit him like a falling tree. Annie was dead. He had her babies to care for.

The babies! He'd left them alone! Panic pushed him to his feet. He yanked open the outside door.

The front entrance of his cabin was open across the way. He heard the voice of a woman singing a familiar Amish hymn. His racing heart slowed as disjointed images from the previous night took shape in his mind.

The babies weren't alone. Annie's sister was

with them. Maisie. Annie's twin. The need to rush and check on his children ebbed away. Seeing them meant seeing Maisie. That painful moment could wait a while longer, but he couldn't put it off forever.

He should have been kinder to Maisie last night. She'd lost her husband in a farming accident before he had married Annie. Maisie knew what it was to lose a spouse. She had moved in with her ailing father on his small farm afterward. Nathan never felt that she'd approved of her sister's choice in marrying a logger with no land or expectations. He could have built a good life in Seymour. If only Annie had stayed.

He raked his hands through his hair. His first uninterrupted night of sleep in nearly a week should have left him refreshed, but it would take more than a single night to get caught up. He yawned, closed his eyes and leaned his head against the doorjamb. He wasn't ready to face the day. Or his new responsibilities as a parent.

What he knew about being a father weighed less than a grain of wheat. It was something he and Annie should have shared together. He barely remembered his own *daed*. He'd died when Nathan was four. A logging accident, his mother had told him. He never knew exactly what happened. She was gone, too, from cancer when he was ten. Now he didn't have anyone he could turn to for guidance. He'd never been more alone.

One of his horses whinnied again. Judging by the height of the sun breaking over the wooded hills to the east, their morning grain was long overdue. He crossed the small room where he had lived last winter. It contained a narrow bed, a table, one chair and a wood-burning potbellied stove. He opened the connecting door that led into his barn. Constructed of logs, the building was small but snug enough to keep his animals comfortable during Maine's long, cold winters. It needed some improvements for sure. He had planned to work on those this summer, but the arrival of the babies had put everything on hold, including his paying job.

Donald and Mack, his caramel-brown Belgians with cream-colored manes, both had their heads over the stall gates gazing in his direction with their ears forward. They knew his arrival meant their grain was imminent. Sassy, his black buggy horse, whickered softly. She was always happy to see him even if he wasn't dishing out food. He stopped to scratch her around the ears. She closed her eyes and leaned into his hand.

"Sorry I'm late again, Sass. I'll figure this out. I promise."

Figure out how to manage his small farm, his logging job and two fussy babies? Sure, he could do that. But first he had to put Maisie on a bus back to Missouri. He didn't need another distraction in his chaotic life.

He fed the horses, his milk cow and her new calf, the pigs, chickens and the ducks, then he cleaned the stalls he had neglected for the past week and gathered the eggs. When he had first arrived at this property he had dammed the small stream that cut through the corner of his pasture to form a pond, where all of the livestock could drink so he didn't have to haul water except during the worst winter months, when it was frozen over.

He had hoped to be able to harvest enough ice from it to fill his icehouse without making the four-mile trip down to the pond at the bishop's place. Instead, heavy spring rains and the runoff from a section of clear-cut forest above him had resulted in a massive amount of silt flowing in. It was little more than a big mudhole now, but his animals could still drink from the deep end. He had planned to drain it and dredge it out, but that would have to wait, along with the other improvements he had hoped to make this summer.

He washed up at the pump outside the cabin and then stared at the open front door. Maisie was still singing. Annie had had a beautiful voice. Maisie's was slightly off-key, but not unpleasant. He didn't hear either baby. The cat was sunning himself on the porch railing while Buddy sprawled across the doorway thumping his tail against the floorboards and licking his chops. The amazing aroma of fresh-baked bread and bacon drifted out and made Nathan's mouth water. His empty stomach gurgled.

There was no point in putting off this meeting any longer. He climbed to the porch and stepped over Buddy to enter the cabin. Maisie stopped singing. She gave him a tentative smile. He had to look away.

"Guder mariye," he mumbled a greeting in Pennsylvania Dutch, the language the Amish spoke among themselves.

"Goot morning to you, too. I hope you got some sleep," she said after an awkward pause.

"I did. What about you?"

Her laugh seemed forced. "I managed. They took turns fussing. As soon as I would get one quiet, the other would wake up wanting attention."

"I noticed that about them." Their baskets were propped on the couch. He stepped over to look at them. They were both asleep. The cabin had rarely been this quiet since their arrival.

Maisie walked up beside him. "Aren't they the most beautiful babies you have ever seen?"

He slanted a glance at her face. Her expression was a mixture of happiness and heart-rending sorrow as she gazed at his children. He almost laid his hand on her shoulder to comfort her but thought better of it.

"I'll get Sassy hitched to the buggy. The trip to Fort Craig takes about an hour."

"I was hoping you would reconsider, Nathan."

He hardened his heart against her pleading look. "I haven't."

She sighed and turned away from him. "Then have some breakfast before your dog snitches more of it. He's not very well trained. He took three strips of bacon off the plate on the counter before I could stop him." She scowled at Buddy, who was doing his best to look innocent.

"He's a stray. I reckon he still worries about where his next meal is coming from."

"I know the feeling," she muttered.

Nathan frowned at her. "What?"

"Nothing. Sit down. *Kaffi?*"

"Sure."

He took a seat and pulled a slice of warm

bread from the plate in the center of the table. The butter melted as he spread it. Maisie filled his white mug with piping-hot coffee, then put the pot back on the stove and brought a plate of bacon and scrambled eggs to the table. She sat down across from him. He kept his eyes closed, said a silent blessing, then picked up his fork.

The eggs were perfectly done and fluffy. The bacon was exactly the way he liked it—not too crisp. The bread was moist and delicious. He took a tentative sip from his mug. It was the best coffee he'd had in months.

He remembered the first breakfast Annie had made for him the day after their wedding. The bacon was burned, the eggs runny and the coffee weak. None of that mattered when she smiled at him. He would have happily eaten charcoal.

He grinned at the recollection. "Remember when—" He looked up and it hit him that it wasn't Annie across from him.

Maisie tipped her head to the side. "Remember what?"

"Never mind." He choked down the rest of the meal and shoved back from the table. He had to get out of the house so he could breathe. He had his hand on the doorknob when Maisie spoke.

"Nathan, wait. Please. Don't make me leave. I'm begging you. Let me care for my sister's babies. They are the only family I have left."

He stood stock-still. "Jacob is gone?"

"*Ja. Daed* passed away three months ago."

"I'm sorry. I didn't know. I liked your father."

"He liked you, too," she said softly. "I don't have family to go back to in Missouri. I had to sell the farm to pay our debts."

He couldn't let sympathy for her loss soften his resolve. He didn't want her here. "You have friends, the members of your church. They'll take care of you."

"I know, but they aren't family."

"I'm sorry. I won't change my mind." The thought of seeing Annie every time he looked at Maisie was more than he could bear. "Be ready to leave in five minutes." He didn't look at her again. His mind was made up.

He hitched Sassy and drove his buggy to the front door. Maisie came out with the twins. He helped settle their baskets on the front seat. She went back inside and returned with her suitcase and a brown paper bag. He stowed her suitcase in the back and nodded toward the bag. "What's that?"

"Formula, diapers, burp rags, clean clothes in case they spit up. You said it was an hour trip so two hours there and back. I'm sure they'll need to be fed and changed before you get them home."

"Right."

She had brought all the things he should have thought of but hadn't. He opened the passenger-side door and helped her in. He closed the door and one of the babies started to fuss. She spoke quietly and gently rocked the basket. The baby settled.

He knew she'd never had children of her own. She and Annie had been the only *kinder* in their family. How did Maisie know so much about taking care of infants? Were women born knowing what to do?

He rubbed his palms on his pant legs. He might not know everything about caring for babies, but he would figure it out. The same way he solved every problem in his life. By trial and error. And by never making the same mistake twice.

"You will stop at the cemetery so I can say my goodbye?" she asked hesitantly.

He had forgotten her request. He glanced toward the small rise behind the house. "She's here."

Maisie's eyes filled with tears as she pressed her fingers to her lips. "Where?"

"I'll show you."

She got out. He took the baby's baskets in each hand. "This way."

He walked up the hill carrying his sleeping infants to a small clearing, where a simple white cross and a mound of dirt marked Annie's final resting place. Maisie sank to the grass beside the grave and laid her hands on the freshly turned earth. She sat in silence with her head bowed.

The morning sun beat down on Nathan's shoulders as he stood behind her. It must have been ten minutes before she sat back and folded her hands in her lap. It struck him that Maisie had always been quieter than Annie, who never could sit still. Maisie had a sereneness about her that Annie had lacked. He found it comforting.

Maisie glanced around and smiled sadly. "It's a lovely spot. It overlooks the cabin. That was a nice thought."

"I'm sorry you came all this way for nothing."

She gazed up at him. His figure against the blue sky was blurred by her unshed tears. "I wish you'd let me stay. Annie wanted me here. She knew how much work two babies could be."

"I'll manage." He avoided looking at her.

She got to her feet and dusted off her hands. "Of course you will. My *daed* used to say you were a problem solver. A man who would think on something before he acted."

He finally glanced at her. "What did your *daed* say about Annie leaving me?"

Maisie bowed her head. "He was ashamed, hurt, confused. He rarely spoke about it."

Nathan stared into the distance. "Did he think I drove her away?"

Maisie laid her hand on his sleeve. "*Nee*, he did not. Nor did I."

She hoped that Nathan believed her because she spoke the truth. Nathan had adored Annie. She knew that.

He shrugged off her hand. "How did Jacob die?"

She clenched her fingers together in her lap. "His heart gave out. I think Annie's leaving took away his will to live. If only she had written. He forgave her. I had to tell her about it when I spoke to her on the phone. I think she took comfort in knowing that." Maisie had hated breaking the news to Annie about their father's death over the phone. She hadn't shared how their father's last days had been spent calling out for Annie and begging to see her.

"Have you forgiven her?" Nathan asked.

"Of course. She was my sister. No matter how poorly she behaved, I loved her."

"We should get going."

They walked back to the buggy, where he settled her and the babies again. He got in on the driver's side and turned the horse to head down the lane. They rode in silence for the first few minutes until his rutted lane met a narrow, paved roadway. It was Maisie who spoke up first. "What is it that you do now, Nathan?"

"The same thing I have always done."

"Logging? Do you have your own business again?"

"*Nee*, I'm a feller for Arthur Davis. He runs most of the lumber camps in this area."

"What exactly is a feller?"

"I'm the man who cuts down trees with a chain saw. I've also worked as a choker, the fellow who hooks cables to the logs so they can be hauled out."

"Is it dangerous work?"

"It can be."

"It must give you peace of mind knowing that your children will be cared for by your Amish community if anything should happen to you."

"I haven't joined the church here. My job often takes me into the backcountry for weeks on end."

"That will have to change now that you have children to look after."

"I know that," he snapped. She fell silent.

Nathan's daughter began to fuss. Maisie picked the child up. She glanced at Nathan's stoic face and tried not to take his rudeness personally. He was suffering and she didn't know how to help him. She patted the baby's back. "I was wondering if you had chosen names yet. I hate to leave without knowing what to call my niece and nephew. I'll want to write to them and send cards at Christmas and such."

"I haven't thought about it."

"Your daughter looks like Annie. Maybe you could name her after her mother."

"Nee." There was no compromise in his tone.

"Well, after your mother, then. What was her name?"

"Charity." His tone softened.

"Charity. I like that. It suits her." Maisie hugged the little girl tightly. At least now she would have a name to add to her prayers.

"It's as good as any," Nathan muttered, but Maisie heard the catch in his voice.

She smiled at the baby trying to get her fist in her mouth. "Hello, Charity Weaver. I'm so very glad I got to meet you."

Nathan glanced at her. "I could call the boy Jacob, after your father, if that's okay with you?"

Maisie swallowed against the lump that formed in her throat. "I'd like that. I think Annie would have, too."

"I'd rather not talk about her."

"I know you are angry, Nathan. None of this is fair, but she was returning to you."

"Why was she coming back? Why did she leave in the first place? Why did she marry me if she didn't love me?"

"I wish I had answers for you."

"I wish you did, too."

They rode in silence until they came to the outskirts of a settlement a half hour later. Off to one side was a school where several dozen Amish children were playing at recess. Most of the children stopped what they were doing to wave. Maisie waved back. "Is this New Covenant?"

"It is."

"So this is where your children will go to school."

"I guess they will someday."

"They will be school-aged before you know it." Maisie looked back at the building as Nathan drove on down the highway. She would be able to imagine the children going up the steps on their first day of school when that day came, playing on the swings, laughing with the other children.

She brushed aside the tears that gathered in her eyes. At least she'd had the chance to hold them and love them, if only for a few hours. It was small consolation compared to the magnitude of her loss, but she was grateful, anyway.

Jacob began to fuss in his basket. Maisie laid Charity down and picked up the bag she'd brought with the formula. She opened a bottle and began to feed him. Before he was finished, Charity began crying. Maisie looked at Nathan. "Pull over, please."

"Why?"

"I can't feed two babies at once. I need you to take Jacob."

Nathan turned off the road into a driveway. A large yellow dog came loping toward them, barking excitedly. An Amish woman tending to her flower garden straightened. She walked over, pulling off her gloves as she came.

"Quiet, Sadie Sue. You'll scare the horse." The dog fell silent but stayed at the woman's heels as she approached the buggy on Maisie's side. "Can I help you?" she asked with a friendly smile.

Maisie handed Jacob to Nathan and picked up Charity. "They both decided they want to eat at the same time. I don't have enough hands."

"Twins. How *wunderbar*." The woman leaned on the door to look inside. "Boys or girls?"

Maisie glanced at Nathan, who seemed intent on ignoring the woman as he got Jacob to finish his bottle. "One of each," Maisie said.

"I'm Bethany Shetler. I don't believe we've met. You must be new to the New Covenant area."

"I'm only visiting. I'm Maisie Schrock. This is my brother-in-law, Nathan Weaver." She nodded to Nathan, who still didn't speak.

"I believe my husband, Michael, mentioned meeting Nathan not long ago. You have the place out beyond the Arnett farm, don't you?"

"I do."

"We haven't seen you at our church services yet."

"That's because I haven't attended one," Nathan said sharply.

Bethany's smile faded. "I see. You are welcome anytime. And you, Maisie, if you are still here on Sunday next."

"He's done with his bottle," Nathan said, settling the baby in his basket again. "We need to get going."

Maisie smiled at the friendly woman and waved goodbye as Nathan turned the buggy onto the highway again.

Neither of them spoke until the outskirts of Fort Craig came into view. On one side of the highway, Maisie noticed several Amish men putting together a small shed on a lot with a half dozen similar buildings.

"Is that an Amish-owned business?" she asked.

"It belongs to Bishop Schultz. He sells garden sheds and such on the side. He's a potato farmer, like most of us. He has a farm near New Covenant."

"It looks like a prosperous business." She took note of several buildings in various stages of completion. One in particular caught her attention. "Is that a little house?"

"The *Englisch* call them tiny homes. Some new fad, I reckon. The bus station is just there."

"Where?"

"In that shopping center."

Her bus driver had dropped her at the New Covenant corner yesterday, so she hadn't been to the one in Fort Craig before. There was a small sign at a convenience store with gas pumps just off the highway. Nathan pulled in and stopped. She got out with one of the babies. Nathan took the other and her suitcase.

They gathered a few curious stares from the patrons in the store as they went in.

Nathan headed to a desk at the end of the room. There wasn't an attendant. A man behind the main counter looked his way. "Be with you folks in a minute."

He finished ringing up a customer and came over. "How can I help you?"

Nathan nodded toward Maisie without looking at her. "My sister-in-law needs a ticket to Seymour, Missouri."

"One way or round trip?" The man sat behind the computer and began typing.

"One way," Nathan said. "How much?"

"It'll take me a few minutes to figure the best way to get you there, ma'am."

Nathan finally looked at her. "Do you have enough money for food on the trip?"

"Ja." Annie had sent money for a round-trip fare. Maisie had spent only part of it getting to Maine.

"Goodbye, then." Nathan put her suitcase on the floor and took Charity's basket from her. He headed for the door. Maisie reached for him. She wasn't ready to say goodbye to the children yet.

"Sir, there isn't a bus going south until Friday afternoon," the ticket agent said quickly, stopping Nathan in his tracks.

"Are you sure?" Maisie asked, her hopes rising.

"Positive. There's a bus going south on Friday afternoons and Monday mornings."

Maisie grinned, almost giddy with relief. She didn't have to leave today. It was only Tuesday. She would have three days to spend with the babies. She glanced at Nathan. He was glaring at her.

Maisie didn't care. She had until Friday to prove to him how much easier his life would be with her help. She glanced at his unyielding expression again. Would that be enough time?

Chapter Three

"This was a wasted morning." Nathan tossed Maisie's suitcase into the back seat of the buggy and climbed in front beside her. She ignored his sour look. She didn't have to leave today. God was good to her.

"Next time I'll stop at the phone shack and call to make sure there is a bus before I drive for a two-hour round trip."

"It doesn't have to be wasted." She was smiling at the babies, not the least bit upset with the turn of events. She couldn't have been happier.

"What do you mean?" he snapped.

"Is there a fabric store in town?"

"Are you joking? You want to make a new dress while you're here?"

Her smile vanished as she turned in the seat to glare at him. "This may not have occurred to you, Nathan Weaver, but your children are in need of clothing."

He leaned away from the anger in her eyes. "What are you talking about?"

"They will soon outgrow the little T-shirts that seem to be all you have for them. I will gladly spend my extra time in Maine sewing for them so they will be comfortable long into the winter months."

She took a deep breath. "I know you are not happy that I will be here until Friday. I'm thrilled that I can spend a few more days with the children, but believe me when I say I am not thrilled to spend that time watching you pout. I can't help that I look like Annie. If you think I'm going to wear a sack over my head to appease you, I won't. You will just have to bear that disappointment."

She crossed her arms tightly over her chest and turned away to stare out the side of the buggy. None of it was her fault and he was acting as if it was.

"I don't want you to wear a sack over your head," he said at last.

He waited for her to say something. She didn't.

"I'm sorry." He opened the door to get out.

"Where are you going?" she asked in a voice that trembled.

"Into the store to see if they know where the closest fabric shop is. And I don't pout."

"You had me fooled."

His eyes narrowed, but he didn't say anything. When he returned to the buggy, he got in and picked up the lines. "There's one down the street."

He drove into the parking lot in front of a shop called Sew Fine. Maisie got out without a word to him.

Inside the door, she was greeted with the smell and sight of stacks of new fabric in a rainbow of colors and prints, button displays, craft items, a bin of quilt square bundles and an elderly clerk who nodded. "Welcome. Just shout if you can't find something."

"Cotton and flannels?"

"End of aisle two, deary."

Maisie picked up a red plastic shopping basket from the stack by the cash register and headed to the back of the store. She paused to look at a solid, royal-blue polyester bolt and walked on. She wasn't shopping for herself. The bolts of flannel were jammed in together at the end of the display. Red plaid seemed to be the most popular, but she chose a few pastel colors. She carried them to the front and left them with the clerk to cut while she went in search of thread and ribbons to make the drawstring closures.

She rounded the end of the aisle and came face-to-face with her sister. Maisie stopped in shock. "Annie?"

She reached out and realized and instant later that she was seeing her own reflection in a full-length mirror on the wall beside ready-made scarves and shawls. It was heartbreaking to see her sister and realize she wasn't real. Tears gathered in Maisie's eyes. She had seldom seen herself in a large mirror. The only one at home had been a small oval one in the bathroom, where her father shaved.

She would never come face-to-face with Annie again. Maisie pressed her hand to her heart. This must be how Nathan saw her. As a painful, unreal reflection of Annie. No wonder he didn't want her to stay.

Out in the buggy, Nathan glanced at the babies and prayed they would stay asleep until Maisie returned. His headache was back. He closed his eyes and leaned his head against the side window. Nothing was going right today. Why hadn't he thought about clothes for the children? They'd need bigger beds soon, too. They couldn't stay in the small Moses baskets the nurses at the hospital had given him. It was all so complicated. Annie should be here to take care of these things.

Twenty minutes later Maisie opened the back door and put several packages on the seat, then she got in front. She appeared subdued. He straightened and cleared his throat. "Now where?"

"A grocery store, if you don't mind. We need more formula and your cupboards are almost bare."

"I wasn't expecting to feed company." He slapped the lines against Sassy's rump to get her moving. Why did he find Maisie so irritating? Annie had never irritated him. She had been easy to get along with. If they had quarreled, he might have understood her leaving, but they never did. Not once. It made her running away that much harder to understand.

He headed Sassy out of town. He passed the local market without stopping. Let Maisie assume he didn't care what she wanted. When they passed the last of the houses along the highway, he glanced at her set face and decided it wasn't worth the energy it took to stay angry with her.

"Mr. Meriwether has a grocery in New Covenant. His prices are a little higher, but he's good to the local Amish who want to sell items at his place. I like to give him my business. In case you were wondering why I didn't turn in at the market back there."

"I was," she admitted softly.

"But you were afraid I'd snap your head off if you asked."

"Something like that." She cast a sidelong glance his way.

He allowed his sour mood to soften. She shouldn't be afraid of him. "I'll try to be less irritated during your remaining days."

A tiny smile tugged at the corner of her lips. "I shall do my best to be less annoying."

As if that was possible. He rubbed the back of his neck with one hand.

Maisie gave him a long look. "Headache?"

He nodded. "*Ja*, I get them when I'm short on sleep."

"Would you like me to drive? You can lie down on the back seat. The fabric bundles will make a decent pillow."

He glanced at her and saw concern in her eyes. For him. Guilt rushed in to push aside his aggravation. He was trying to get rid of her, and she was worried about his comfort. He shook his head. "I'll be fine, but *danki*."

"As you wish." She turned away.

When they arrived at the Meriwether Market, he pulled in and stopped. "Let me give you some money." He pulled out his wallet.

Her chin came up. "I have enough. I don't wish to be a burden."

"I will pay for what the babies and you need while you are here. Keep in mind I only have a small icebox, so don't get a lot of perishable items."

"Of course." She took his money, got out and entered the store.

Nathan massaged his neck again. His headache hadn't let up. It probably wouldn't go away until Maisie left.

Charity began to fuss. He reached over and gently rocked the basket as he had seen Maisie do. Thankfully, his daughter quieted. He wondered how long it would be before both babies slept through the night. A few weeks? Surely not more than that. He had been so overwhelmed during the first few days with them that he hadn't had time to consider what he was going to do about work.

He would need to find someone to take care of them eventually. Arthur Davis had been good about giving him time off. He had offered Nathan a month's leave, but without pay, since the other feller on the crew was experienced enough to handle the extra workload alone. Nathan hated to ask for more time, but he might have to if he couldn't find someone quickly.

He rubbed his tense neck again. Having Maisie to help would have worked, if only she wasn't the spitting image of Annie. He didn't need the added pain.

Charity squirmed in her sleep. Maisie's suggestion for his daughter's name had been a good one, though. His mother would have loved having babies to spoil. God had taken her and Annie much too soon. The Lord hadn't shown Nathan Weaver much mercy in his life.

Jacob stirred. Nathan rocked him until he settled. It wasn't so hard to care for them now that he knew what to do. Nathan sat back feeling pleased with himself. Then Charity started crying.

"I have heard that your goods are overpriced. Now I see that's true." Maisie kept a close watch on the cash register's rising total. She would show Nathan she knew how to manage money. She was a thrifty shopper.

"My prices are fair." The middle-aged man scowled at her as he rang up the container of powdered formula.

"This is at least a dollar higher than the last place I saw the same formula."

"There was a coupon for it in this week's newspaper. If you have one of those, I'll take a dollar off what you have here."

"I'm afraid I didn't see the newspaper. I'm newly arrived." She smiled at him. "Couldn't you give me the discount, anyway? The twins are going to need a lot of formula over the next few months."

He brightened at the prospect of future sales. "Twins, you say. What a blessing. All right, I will give you the discount. Keep an eye on my ads in the newspaper. You'll find some good bargains, I promise."

"*Danki*, you're very kind. The last place I lived the Amish women would travel together once a month to shop at a large discount store even though it was twenty miles away. Do the Amish women in this community do that?"

"I've not heard of it." His frown came back.

"Perhaps I'll suggest it." She cast a sidelong glance his way to gauge his reaction.

He finished scanning her items. "I'm going to deduct five percent from the total. That's my way of welcoming you to the community."

She smiled broadly. "That's very generous of you."

And a good way to appease a troublesome customer.

"Well, folks are glad to have the Amish moving in here. My grandparents were potato farmers back in the day. They worked the land with horses the way you folks do. The old ways shouldn't disappear. Why, I can remember riding bareback on Grandpa's plow horse. His name was Dusty, which was exactly the way the seat of my pants looked when I got off of him."

Maisie grinned as she handed over her money. "Happy memories are cherished gifts from *Gott*."

"They are indeed." He counted out her change and picked up two of the bags. "Let me help you out with these."

"Danki."

The moment they stepped out the door, Maisie heard the babies crying.

Mr. Meriwether chuckled. "It sounds as if you'll need some of that formula right quick. I'll put these sacks in the back for you." He opened the door and nodded to Nathan. "Your missus knows how to drive a good bargain. I was afraid I was going to have to pay her to take these groceries off my hands."

"I'm his sister-in-law and thank you again for the help, Mr. Meriwether."

The man left and Maisie opened the front door of the buggy. Nathan had a babe in each arm, trying to soothe them. A worried frown creased his brow. "I can't believe they are hungry already. Is something else wrong with them?"

"The long ride in the buggy may have upset them, but it's been almost three hours since we stopped to feed them. That's about normal. Let me have Charity. I'll change her and then you can feed her while I take care of Jacob. These are for you." She opened a bottle of aspirin and shook two into her hand, then laid a bottle of water on the seat.

He handed the babe to her and she dropped the pills into his free hand. He quickly tossed them in his mouth and took a swig of water. "*Danki.* How do you know they aren't sick?"

She laid the back of her hand against Charity's forehead. "She doesn't have a fever. I'm sure a dry diaper and a bottle will stop the fussing."

That turned out to be the case. Once both babies were changed and fed, Maisie held one in each arm, enjoying the time to cuddle them as Nathan drove toward home.

"How is it that you know so much about babies?" he asked.

"I worked as a nanny for an *Englisch* family." Annie had worked in the same house as a maid.

"The Porters." Nathan's tone conveyed his lingering dislike of the wealthy family that had caused him so much trouble. Edward Porter, the head of the family, had treated Nathan poorly.

"Gavin Porter, the son, had two children. His wife was sickly. I took care of her baby and two-year-old son until I left to get married."

Annie had stayed on and taken over Maisie's duties with the children. Gavin and Annie became close. Maisie had worried about her sister's attachment. She suspected Annie was in love with Gavin. Because he was a married man and Annie had already taken her baptismal vows, any romantic relationship between them was strictly forbidden. Then Maisie's husband died suddenly in an accident, leaving her with the farm to run. Between the farm work and their father's failing health, Maisie had been too busy to do or say anything about her concerns.

After Gavin's wife passed away, he moved with the children to New York. Then Annie suddenly married Nathan, a newcomer, an Amish logger she'd known only a few months. Annie's assurance that she had fallen madly in love didn't ring true to Maisie. She thought her sister was marrying Nathan help her get over Gavin. To prove she hadn't been in love with him.

"I'm surprised the Porters hired someone without experience as their nanny."

"When I was younger, I worked as a mother's helper for our neighbor after she had two of her children. She gave me a reference."

"Old man Porter took the word of an Amish *frau*? That's not like him."

"It was Gavin who hired me." Maisie had enjoyed taking care of the children. When she married, she thought she would have babes of her own, but that wasn't God's plan for her.

She gazed at the beautiful babies sleeping quietly in her arms and her heart grew warm with tenderness. It was astonishing how quickly she had grown to love them. Three days wasn't much time to prove her worth to Nathan, but the idea of leaving Annie's babies was too painful to contemplate.

She would show Nathan that she was the perfect nanny for his children. She rocked gently with the swaying of the buggy watching their changing expressions in their sleep, feeling them stretch and snuggle inside their blankets. Even when her arms grew tired, she didn't put them down. Every moment with them was precious.

"How soon will they start sleeping through the night?" Nathan asked, glancing in her direction.

"When they are five or six months old."

"That can't be right."

"I'm afraid it is."

He looked so disappointed that she felt sorry for him. She decided not to tell him about colic, teething, croup or any of the other reasons parents of new babies lost sleep. Today didn't seem to be the day to add to his worries.

When they finally arrived back at his cabin, he got out of the buggy, came around to her side and opened her door. She grimaced when she tried to move. "I'm sorry, can you take Jacob? I'm afraid my arms have fallen asleep."

"You should've put them down sooner." He leaned close to gently lift the baby from her arms.

"I didn't want to miss a minute of holding them while I'm able. They are so beautiful. Truly a gift from *Gott*."

He paused with his gaze fixed on his son's face. He stroked the baby's cheek with one finger. "They are wonderful. I wish their mother was here to see how much they've changed in just a few days' time."

"So do I, but it was *Gott*'s will." She shook her arm to clear the pins and needles, then stepped out of the buggy. Nathan took her elbow to steady her. Warmth spread from his hand up her arm. Her gaze flew to his face. A troubled expression clouded his eyes.

He stepped away abruptly. "Go inside. I'll bring the baskets."

Maisie did as he asked. She waited in the kitchen until he set the baskets on the table. She laid Charity in one and he placed Jacob in the other. Then he stood back and slipped his hands into his pockets.

"Oh, I almost forgot," Maisie said. "Here is your change." She pulled the money out of her purse.

Nathan took the bills, counted them and slipped them in his wallet. "You didn't use much. Did you spend your own money?"

"*Nee*. I was able to find some bargains. I'm careful with money." She took off her black traveling bonnet and laid it on the counter.

"Mr. Meriwether said as much. I thought it was just flattery."

Nathan went outside and returned a few minutes later with her purchases. He set them on the counter without looking at her. "I must see to Sassy. Then I have work in the barn. Don't bother fixing me anything to eat."

"You can't go hungry because I'm here. I'll fix you something now."

"I said, don't bother," he snapped and left again. Maisie sank onto the kitchen chair. How could she prove her worth if he couldn't stay in the same room with her?

"Annie, you really hurt that man. Each time he looks at me I see the anguish in his eyes. You wanted me to be here, but you've made it impossible for me to stay."

She leaned forward to look at the sleeping babies. "I'll take good care of your *kinder* for as long as I'm able."

Maisie heard the sounds of a chain saw and an axe throughout the afternoon. Nathan didn't come in again until it was nearly dark. She'd kept a pot of stew warm on the stove for him, but the canned meat and vegetables were overdone and mushy by the time he showed up. He stopped to kiss each of the sleeping babies and then went out again. She fed the stew to Buddy.

The next morning, Nathan came in, poured himself a cup of coffee and went back out. Maisie ate some of the scrambled eggs she had made and gave the rest to Buddy and the cat. Nathan's animals would soon be fat at this rate. It wasn't long before she heard the chain saw again. Later, the banging of a hammer came from beyond the barn.

Just after noon, the sound of a vehicle coming up the lane prompted her to go to the door and look out. A brown pickup pulled into the small farmyard and stopped. She saw the words *Davis Lumber Company* on the truck door in white letters. A burly *Englisch* man in his midfifties got out. He wore faded jeans held up with suspenders, a blue plaid shirt and a brown baseball cap with the same company name stitched in white letters across the front.

He caught sight of her and pulled off his cap. "Afternoon, ma'am. I'm Arthur Davis. I'm looking for Nathan."

"I'm his sister-in-law, Maisie Schrock. I think Nathan is in the barn."

The man tipped his head slightly. "I don't recall Nathan saying he had any family."

"His wife was my sister."

"Then I'm sure sorry for your loss."

"Thank you."

"But I'm mighty glad to see he has someone to help with the babies."

"Would you like to come in for some coffee? I was just about to put on a pot."

"No thanks. I'll just go speak to Nathan." Mr. Davis started to turn away, but Nathan was already coming in their direction.

"I wasn't expecting you, Mr. Davis. What can I do for you?"

"There's been an accident at the Three Ponds camp. Ricky Burris broke his leg when a widow-maker came down on him."

"I'm sorry to hear that. Is he going to be okay?"

"The doc said he'd be off at least two months.

With your situation, I was already short one feller and now I've got none. Could you see your way to come back to work starting on Monday? I know it's short notice. I wouldn't ask, but the lumber is already contracted for and I can't get behind schedule."

Nathan stared at his feet. He scuffed the toe of one boot through the gravel. "Things aren't settled here."

"I know it's bad timing on my part, and I hate to say it, but I'm gonna have to hire two new fellers to get this project in on time if you aren't willing to return to work."

Nathan looked up sharply. "Two? Are you telling me that I'm out of a job if I don't come back now?"

"The last thing I want to do is lay you off, Nathan, but I have obligations, too. I wanted to give you the opportunity to come back before I did anything. If Ricky hadn't gotten hurt I could've spared you for a few weeks, but not longer than that."

The man turned his hat around in his hands. "Look, I don't need your answer today. I'll give you some time to think it over. I'm really sorry to do this to you. You're the best feller I've had in a long time and I don't want to lose you. Think it over and let me know tomorrow. I'll stop by in the morning."

Mr. Davis settled his hat on his head, got in his truck and drove away.

Maisie wished she could do something for Nathan. He didn't need more trouble than he already had. She walked over to stand beside him. "What are you going to do?"

"There's no way I can make it through the winter with the savings I've got left after I pay the medical bills for the twins and Annie. I need my job."

"Your church will help you pay the hospital costs."

"They might if I was a member of this church. Which I'm not. I'll have to hire someone quickly to take care of the babies so I can go back to work."

He didn't even glance at her when he said it. She couldn't believe what she was hearing. He would rather employ a stranger to look after his children than allow his wife's sister to be their nanny. The man wasn't thinking straight.

Maisie planted her hands on her hips. "Whether you like it or not, I'm staying. Those babies need me, not some stranger."

Chapter Four

"You can't stay here," Nathan snapped, wishing she would go away.

If she'd stay out of his sight instead of harping at him, he could think of what to do next. Annie had never been this exasperating. "You have a bus ticket you need to use on Friday."

Maisie stood with her hands on her hips and a stubborn look simmering in her eyes. "And you have to give your boss an answer tomorrow. Allow me to stay. What's your alternative?"

He didn't have one and he hated being backed into a corner. "Your sister was a biddable woman. I can see that you aren't."

Maisie folded her arms tightly over her chest. "We might have been twins, but we weren't the same."

Nathan didn't want to argue with her. His head was killing him. "I'm going to see Bishop

Schultz. He may know of a woman who can look after the children." He was grasping at straws and he knew it. Finding someone to care for the babies full-time on such short notice was unlikely.

Maisie tossed her hands up. "Why are you so stubborn?"

"They're my children. I say who takes care of them." He started to walk away.

"You're being unreasonable."

"Enough." He raised one hand to signal the end of the conversation and kept walking.

"You're obstinate and irrational! No wonder my sister left you," she shouted.

Nathan stopped as pain seared his heart. He hung his head and gripped it with both hands. He'd gone over it a million times. There was only one explanation for Annie's actions. She left because there was something wrong with him. There was some reason she couldn't love him.

He heard Maisie running toward him. "Nathan, I'm sorry," she said in a rush.

She stopped beside him, but he couldn't look at her. He could barely breathe.

"That was cruel of me," she said softly. "You didn't deserve it."

His throat was so tight he couldn't speak.

Maisie laid a hand on his arm. "I'm sorry.

Please forgive me. My temper is a fault I've tried to overcome."

He cleared the lump in his throat and found his voice. "You need to work on it harder," he croaked.

She let her breath out in a rush. "I will, I promise. I don't know why I said that. She never spoke a word against you, Nathan. Never."

He stared at the sky and blinked back tears. "I wish she had. Then maybe I'd understand. I'm just so tired and…"

"Angry. I know. I am, too, Nathan. I'm angry with *Gott* for taking her from me just when we had the chance to become close again. I'm angry with Annie for hurting you. For wounding me and our father. And for leaving her babies, though I know she couldn't help it. None of it was your fault." She tightened her grip on his arm. "Nothing gives me the right…to hurt you."

The catch in her words made him look at her. Tears streamed down her face. Her pain was as great as his own. Almost against his will, he cupped his fingers under her chin and gently wiped the dampness from one cheek with his thumb. "I reckon we're both grieving. They say healing takes time."

She nodded mutely.

Her skin was soft and warm beneath his

fingers. Old longings shuddered to life in his chest. The need to hold someone and to be held. He knew the curve of this woman's jaw and the softness of her lips, but the woman whose face he caressed wasn't his wife. His feelings were for Annie, and she was gone. Maisie was only her shadow. Any warmness she stirred in him wasn't real.

More than the woman he had buried on the hill, he mourned the loss of the sweet girl he had married. The one who had left him months ago. His love for her had died a slow and painful death until there was only a hollow where his heart used to be.

How could he heal with Maisie as a constant reminder of all he had lost? It wasn't possible. He let his hand fall to his side. "I don't know where you and your sister learned to be so cruel, but I forgive you. I'll be home late. Don't wait supper."

Maisie stepped back and wiped her cheeks as much to hide the flush that heated her face as to dry her tears. Her reaction to Nathan's touch surprised and shocked her. She struggled to sound unaffected. "I'll keep something warm for you."

"Don't trouble yourself." He walked away and entered the barn.

Maisie relaxed when he was out of sight. Had he noticed the way her breath caught in her throat at the touch of his fingers? She hoped not. He had only been comforting her. It was her ragged emotions that made it seem like his touch had meant something more. She dismissed her troubled thoughts as a product of too little sleep and raw grief. To imagine there could be anything between Nathan and herself was utter foolishness. She knew better. He could barely stand the sight of her.

Now he thought she was as cruel as Annie, and she hadn't given him cause to think otherwise.

She looked up at the sky. "I'm ashamed of myself, Lord. My sorrow at Annie's death is no excuse for my words. I will do better. Give me a chance to mend my mistakes and help me bring Nathan the comfort he needs. I pray you fill my heart with kindness and hold my tongue when I would speak ill. Nathan has suffered enough because of my sister. Don't let me add to his pain. I can't change how I look, but with your guidance I can change how I act."

Walking back to the house, Maisie gave silent thanks for God's grace in allowing her to enjoy more time with the babies.

Nathan drove the buggy out of the barn and went past her. She watched him until he was out of sight. God willing, she might have even more time with them. It was wrong to hope that Nathan's mission would prove fruitless, but she couldn't help it. She didn't want to leave. The babies needed her, and Nathan needed her, too.

Inside the cabin she walked over to the sofa, where Charity and Jacob were still sleeping. Buddy was sitting alertly in front of them. He wagged his tail as Maisie sat down beside him.

"You are a *goot hund* to watch over your charges so well." His tail wagged faster. She scratched behind his long floppy ear, and he licked her hand.

"At least you are glad to have me here."

With a final pat to the dog's shoulder, she got up and began heating water on the stove to wash the glass bottles and nipples she had purchased. After that, she made up enough formula to get through the night, then put the bottles in Nathan's small icebox.

In her Amish community in Missouri they were allowed to use propane-powered appliances, so she was used to a bigger refrigerator. There wasn't any fresh milk in the icebox. She didn't know if Nathan owned a milk cow, so she had purchased canned milk that didn't need refrigeration for her cooking along with a variety of canned meats.

Did he have a garden? She had been too focused on Annie's grave yesterday morning to notice anything else on his property. With both babies asleep, now would be a good time to explore.

She stepped outside. Buddy refused to budge from his place in front of the sofa. She closed the door and took a long look around.

Nathan's cabin was situated in a clearing surrounded by dense forest. Mostly pine trees interspersed with hardwoods. The log barn stood at the edge of a fenced-in meadow. She could see a pond at the far end with half a dozen white ducks swimming in it. Looking in the other direction, she knew what lay on the knoll above the cabin. She wasn't up to another visit there yet.

She went around to the back and was pleased to discover Nathan did have a garden, although it was somewhat overgrown. There were even a dozen young fruit trees, carefully wrapped and staked. The start of his orchard. He had accomplished a lot since leaving Missouri.

White cloth diapers flapped on a short clothesline attached to the corner of the house, but she didn't see a washer on the small back porch. Did Nathan wash his clothes by hand? The diapers were dry so she gathered them off the line.

She found his potato patch and dug enough new potatoes to make a soup later with some of the canned ham she had picked up. She spent the next twenty minutes pulling weeds and gathering what vegetables were ripe. At the far end of the garden she saw a huge blueberry bush. It had clearly been there for years. It was wild or someone had planted it long ago. The berries weren't ripe, but there would be plenty for jams and pie filling when they were.

If only she could be here to harvest them.

After checking on the babies, she went down to the barn. Curiosity made her peek into the room where Nathan had spent the last two nights. It was small but neat. His bed was made. No clothes hung from the pegs and the stove was cold.

Through the interior door, she found Mack and Donald dozing in their stalls. A brown-and-white cow occupied another stall. She had a tiny calf nursing at her side. Maisie leaned over the stall door for a closer look. "I see why Nathan doesn't have fresh milk in his icebox. He's letting your baby have it all."

The calf didn't pause in her feeding, but the cow followed Maisie's every move watchfully.

A chicken was scratching dirt in the corner of the cow's stall. Nathan had brought in eggs that morning, so he had to have several chickens. It didn't take her long to find where the others were sitting in their boxes. She left them undisturbed and returned to the house.

Inside the snug cabin, Maisie sat at the table and looked around. The furniture wasn't fancy. The table and chairs were homemade, from what looked like local wood. The one brown overstuffed chair was well-worn. The sofa was secondhand—that was easy to see—but all in all Nathan had made a good home in Maine.

Would Annie have been happy here? Maisie wasn't so sure. Hewing a living out of the wilderness would be challenging. Annie hadn't been one for hard work. She had been better at getting others to do her work for her.

It was wrong to think of her sister's faults when she'd passed so recently. Maisie wanted to remember the good times, the fun they'd had together. Those were the stories she would tell the children about their mother when they were older, even if only in the letters she wrote to them.

She took a deep breath and began to tidy up. She dusted the furniture, polished the reflective discs behind the oil lamps on the stone fireplace mantel and cleaned their sooty shades. Then she swept and washed the plank floor with a pine-scented cleaner she found under the kitchen sink.

Afterward, she fixed supper for herself, then fed and bathed the babies. She laughed at their startled expressions, and again when she was splashed by Jacob's wildly kicking legs. Once they were settled, she found a book about gardening in Maine from the stack of reading material beside Nathan's overstuffed chair. She sat in the kitchen reading by the light of a kerosene lantern and waited for Nathan to come home. She heard the horse and buggy about an hour after dark. Nathan didn't come in. Was he still upset with her? What had he learned?

She put some of the leftover soup she had kept warm on the back of the stove into a mug, fixed a ham sandwich and carried them down to the barn. Gathering her courage, she knocked on his door. When he opened it, she thrust the covered plate toward him. "It's just a bit of soup and a sandwich in case you haven't eaten."

He hesitated for so long that she thought he would refuse, but he finally reached out and took the dish. *"Danki."*

He looked bone tired. She crossed her arms over her chest. "Do you have another headache?"

He walked over to his cot. "It's manageable. How are the babies?"

She smiled. "Manageable. Jacob loved his bath."

Nathan's eyes brightened. "Did he?"

"He kicks like a little frog."

Nathan sat on the foot of his cot. Maisie stayed in the doorway. Her smile faded. "Did the bishop know of someone you can hire?"

"He will ask around. He didn't know of anyone offhand." Nathan took a sip of soup.

"You could put an ad in the newspaper." Maisie clamped her lips shut. Why was she helping find her own replacement?

Because she wanted to help Nathan, as well as the children. She turned to leave but he spoke. "This is *goot*."

"I'm glad you like it."

"I'll come see the babies before I turn in."

She smiled softly and leaned her shoulder against the doorjamb. "Of course. You'll have to get past Buddy. He's appointed himself their guardian."

"Is that so? All he did before you came was howl when they cried."

"Perhaps he's gotten used to them. Have you decided what you're going to tell your boss?"

He took another sip of soup before answering. "I'll go back to work. I don't have much choice. It's not what I want. I need to take care of my children. They are my responsibility. I should be the one looking after them."

"Nathan, I'm not trying to take that away from you."

He glanced at her sharply. "Aren't you?"

"I'm not. You're their father. I am only their aunt. Because I love them that doesn't diminish how much you love them." She tried to understand what was going on behind his hooded expression. "They won't love you any less because I'm here."

He stared at his sandwich without commenting.

Maisie sighed. "Come up to the house whenever you're ready." She walked back to the cabin in the darkness.

Nathan set his unfinished food aside. Was that what he was afraid of? That his son and his daughter wouldn't love him if there was someone else in their lives? Was he frightened of being abandoned again? Was he that selfish? That insecure?

How could Maisie guess what he was feeling when he didn't know it himself? Despite her temper and her stubbornness, she was a perceptive woman.

Weariness dragged at him and made him want to lie down and cover his head, but he couldn't sleep until he knew his babies were okay. He forced himself to get to his feet and walk up to the cabin.

Light spilled out the open doorway with a welcoming warmth. He stepped inside and paused. Everything was clean and brighter. The cobwebs were gone from the corners. His floor hadn't looked this good since he'd first laid it. The whole place smelled fresh.

He didn't see Maisie. The Moses baskets were on the sofa. Buddy lay sprawled across the floor in front of them. He got up when Nathan moved toward him. Nathan patted the dog's head and smiled at the sight of his children sleeping peacefully. He looked down at the dog. "They are a lot sweeter when they're quiet, aren't they?"

Nathan took one of the kitchen chairs, turned it around and placed it beside the babies. He leaned forward with his arms braced on the back of it and just watched them. Charity's eyebrows wiggled up and down as if she was trying to open her eyes. Jacob gave a small grunt and then smiled. His tiny hands grasped at the blanket. Nathan reached down and let his son wrap his small hand around his index finger. The boy's grip was amazing for his size.

He heard a sound behind him. Glancing over his shoulder, he saw Annie had come in. He realized his mistake an instant later and looked away. Maisie walked up to him. "You may hold them if you wish."

"I don't want to wake them."

"Babies need to be held."

"If you insist." It was what he needed, and somehow she knew it. Nathan reached down and scooped up his son. He settled him in the crook of his arm. The boy stretched but didn't wake.

Nathan sat in awe of the gifts he had been given. Annie had taken a lot from him, but she had given him something immeasurably precious in the end. He could feel his anger toward her shrinking. It wasn't gone, but it wasn't as painful to think about.

"I've been told that babies like the sound of familiar voices," Maisie said.

He glanced at her for the first time without resentment. "You mean just talk? What should I say?"

"You can tell him about your day or read something."

"I don't have any children's storybooks."

She sat down on the sofa beside Charity. "You don't have to read from a book. You can read from a magazine or from the Bible. Anything that sounds soothing."

"Maybe I'll just talk about my day."

He concentrated on Jacob's face. "Today wasn't the best of days. I went all the way to Fort Craig on a wild-goose chase to catch a bus that wasn't there. My boss stopped in to see me to tell me I will lose my job if I can't tear myself away from you and your sister. It was a tough decision, but I have to earn a living for you. Then I had an argument with your aunt. After that I went on another wild-goose chase to find a nanny and came back empty-handed."

He glanced at Maisie from the corner of his eye. Her eyes were downcast and her face was flushed. Embarrassment? He looked back at Jacob. "The best part of the whole day was a cup of yummy potato-and-ham soup that your aunt Maisie made for me."

He leaned down and whispered just loud enough for her to hear, "Maybe she'll leave us the recipe before she goes home if we ask nicely."

Jacob smiled in his sleep and Nathan smiled back at him.

"You left out the part where their bad-tempered auntie gave you a roaring headache," Maisie said.

Nathan realized his headache was almost gone. "I'm saving that part for tomorrow evening."

He stood up, kissed Jacob's forehead and

laid him in his basket. Then he leaned down and kissed Charity's soft, plump cheek. "Sleep well, *liebling*, my little love."

He thrust his hands in his pockets as he faced Maisie. "I can take them down to my room for the night if you want some rest."

"I'm fine. We can trade off tomorrow night if you wish." The look was back in her eyes. The one that pleaded with him to change his mind and let her stay on.

He ignored it and walked to the door. He stopped and turned to her. "The place looks nice."

"Danki." She seemed surprised by his compliment.

He was a little shocked that he'd said anything, too. "Plan on staying until the bus leaves next Friday." Surely he could find someone to look after the children in a week's time.

The joy on her face took his breath away. She clasped her hands together as she smiled at him. "Bless you, Nathan."

"Don't expect to stay longer." He assumed her smile would dim, but it didn't. She nodded, but he suspected she was already thinking of ways to extend her stay.

He walked out into the night. Why had he been moved by the sight of her happiness? Because it was like seeing Annie happy again. That was all it was.

Yet something about that assumption didn't feel right.

Opening the door to his room, he stopped and looked at his narrow bed and the half-eaten supper beside it. It was quiet without the babies, but lonely. He'd lived with loneliness for months. Why should it feel different now?

He sat down and finished the cold soup, then ate his sandwich. Through the window he saw the lights in the cabin go out. Suddenly he wished he hadn't told Maisie she could stay longer. She was too unsettling to have around. The best woman for the job would be older. A grandmotherly person. Not someone with bright green eyes that silently pleaded for him to change his mind whenever he looked her way. Definitely not a woman who sensed things about him that he didn't know himself.

If the bishop didn't find someone, Nathan would use Maisie's suggestion and advertise the position in the local paper. It didn't have to be Amish women.

He realized he didn't need to wait on the bishop. He could place the ad and put up flyers in the grocery store and other local businesses. He'd do it in the morning.

Feeling better with a plan in place, he blew

out the lamp and lay back in bed with his arms crossed behind his head. Maisie wasn't staying a moment longer than necessary. Not if he could help it. He wouldn't let her imploring eyes change his mind.

Chapter Five

Maisie was humming when Nathan entered the cabin early the next morning. Was she always such a cheerful soul? The smell of fresh-baked bread filled the air with an enticing aroma that made his stomach rumble. She opened his finicky stove and pulled out two beautiful golden-brown loaves. She must've been up for hours. Did the woman even need sleep?

When she turned around, he saw the answer to his question. There were dark circles under her eyes.

"Was it a rough night?" he asked.

"A little," she admitted. "They started fussing after midnight and kept it up until about an hour ago. I wonder if the different formula doesn't agree with them?"

He frowned. "How will we know?"

"They'll continue to fuss after they eat until they get used to it. If they stay fussy on it, I'll have to change back to what the hospital sent home with you. Go ahead and sit down. Your breakfast is ready. I made scrambled eggs. I hope that's okay."

"I like dippy eggs better, but that's fine." He liked to soak his bread in the runny yolks, but he wasn't going to turn down scrambled ones that he didn't have to fix himself.

He took a seat. She wrapped her apron around one of the loaves and carried it to the table. When she sliced it open, steam rose in a fragrant cloud. His mouth started watering. He loved hot, fresh bread.

Maisie pressed her hands to the small of her back and leaned backward with a grimace. Then she returned to the stove to dish up the eggs and bring over the coffeepot. She filled his cup and then her own. Leaving it on a pot holder in the center of the table, she sat down, folded her hands and bowed her head.

He prayed silently, as he had been taught by his mother, and cleared his throat when he was finished. Maisie immediately reached for her coffee. Before she got the cup to her mouth, one of the babies began crying. "Oh, dear. That's Jacob."

He wondered how she could tell just from

the sound of the child's cry. She took one sip and put her cup aside. She started to rise but Nathan forestalled her. "I'll see to him."

She shook her head. "Your breakfast will get cold."

He pushed back from the table. "I've had many a cold meal. Drink your *kaffi*. You look like you could use it."

"No flattery from you this morning."

"You should be glad I didn't say what I was thinking."

She rolled her eyes. "That I look like a worn-out hag?"

"Those are your own words."

"If I look as bad as I feel, they're accurate."

He picked up Jacob and settled him upright against his chest, then sat at the table again. Between patting the baby's back and making soothing sounds, he managed to fork eggs into his mouth with his free hand. Buddy had followed him and stood by Nathan's chair whining softly.

Jacob belched and spit up on Nathan's shoulder. He grimaced as the wet soaked through his shirt. "I reckon that was his problem."

Maisie was out of her chair and getting a kitchen towel before he could say anything else. He shifted the baby to his other shoulder while she dabbed at his shirt. He finally took the towel from her. "It's just a little sour milk. Don't fuss."

"I can take him." She held out her arms.

"He's fine where he is. Sit."

Buddy promptly sat and stopped whining. Maisie returned to her chair. Nathan glanced at his dog and then at Maisie. "That's better. Could you butter a piece of bread for me?"

"Of course." She quickly slathered a slice and handed it to him. He fed it to the dog.

"What are you doing?" she asked in astonishment.

"I'm rewarding the dog for doing as he was told even if I wasn't talking to him."

She clamped her lips together. He arched one eyebrow. "You don't approve?"

"He's your dog." She picked up her coffee cup again. "He will never stop begging at the table if you feed him from it."

"Are you an expert on dogs as well as on babies?"

"Not at all. We never allowed our dogs in the house," she said primly.

He looked at his hound. "Did you hear that, Buddy? She might feel differently when it's thirty below outside and she's in bed with cold feet."

Her mouth dropped open, but she quickly snapped it shut. "I would rather get another quilt than allow a flea-bitten mongrel into my bed."

"Buddy doesn't have fleas, do you, boy? I put a little vinegar in his water and that takes care of them."

"Good to know." She propped her elbow on the table and settled her chin on her palm. Her eyelids began to drift lower. She jerked awake, blinked several times and then settled into the same position.

He wondered if she was going to fall asleep in her scrambled eggs. He knew how exhausting taking care of the twins could be. He had enjoyed an uninterrupted night and decided she deserved a break. He shoveled in his last forkful of eggs, washed them down with coffee and got to his feet. "I'm going to take the twins down to the barn with me this morning."

Her head popped up. "What?"

"I'm going to watch the children for a while. I suggest you use the free time to catch up on some sleep."

"I'm fine. I can look after them."

There was that pleading look again.

He hardened his heart against it. "So can I."

Rather than arguing, he simply laid Jacob on his bed and picked up both baskets. He walked to the door. "Come on, Buddy."

The dog happily went out the door ahead

of him. Nathan looked over his shoulder at Maisie. "I appreciate you making breakfast. Get some rest. You need it." He pulled the door closed and stared at it.

He shouldn't have said that, but she looked so worn out that he had taken pity on her. He didn't want to encourage her or give her false hope. He wasn't going to change his mind. Maisie was going to be on the first available bus as soon as he found a *kinder heeda*.

Maisie managed a tired smile. If he appreciated her cooking, that was a start. Maybe he was relenting.

Your words made my sleepless night worthwhile, Nathan Weaver. Danki.

She considered starting on some new clothes for the twins but realized she couldn't keep her eyes open long enough to set the stitches. She climbed the steps to the loft so she could lie down. The pillow held Nathan's scent. It was comforting and it made her feel closer to him.

She only needed to rest her eyes for a few minutes and then she would be fine.

Sometime later she heard crockery clattering in the kitchen. She sat up and looked over the low knee wall that ran the length of the open loft. Nathan was finishing the dishes. The babies were fast asleep in their beds on the sofa.

Buddy sat beside Nathan at the kitchen counter, watching him hopefully. How long had she been asleep?

"What time is it?" she asked.

Nathan looked up and then quickly glanced away. "Half past noon. I'm fixing church spread. Would you like some on a slice of bread?"

He still couldn't look at her. Maisie sighed. Her resemblance to her sister was an obstacle she couldn't overcome.

"That sounds *wunderbar.*" She patted her *kapp* to make sure it was on straight, then went down the steep stairs to the kitchen.

He held out a plate without looking at her. She took it and crossed to the sofa, where she sat beside Charity. The church spread, a peanut-butter-and-marshmallow cream spread, was delicious on a thick slice of her homemade bread. She licked her fingers when she was finished. Nathan stood at the sink gazing out the window while he ate. Occasionally, he broke off a piece and fed it to the dog.

"Has Mr. Davis been by?" Her voice sounded strained to her own ears.

"He stopped in."

She waited for more information, but Nathan wasn't forthcoming. "And? What did you tell him?"

He continued to stare out the window. "I told him to put me on the schedule for Monday. Now that you're up I am going into town." He turned around but only to grab some papers and his hat from the table. He stopped in the open doorway but didn't look back. "Do you need anything?"

A sack to wear over my head so that you can look at me and not see Annie.

No doubt he would be happy to bring her one. "Nothing, *danki.*"

"I don't know when I'll be back. If you need anything the phone shack is about a quarter of a mile south of the end of my lane. Lilly Arnett's phone number is on the wall. She's the closest neighbor. She'll help." He went out the door without waiting for her reply.

Maisie gazed at the sleeping babies. "At least he isn't so angry today. Your *daed* won't admit it, but he can't ignore me forever."

She got up and began sorting her fabric. She had finished cutting out a pair of gowns for the babies when she heard a buggy pull up outside about an hour later. She assumed it was Nathan so she didn't go to the door. She was startled to hear women's voices outside.

She put her sewing aside as two Amish women appeared in the doorway. "Hello, sister," the older one said. "May we come in?"

Shocked to have visitors, Maisie sprang to her feet. "Of course. I'm sorry but Nathan has gone into town."

The two middle-aged women smiled brightly as they glanced about at the interior of the cabin. "What a snug little home Nathan Weaver has built," the one with wire-rimmed spectacles said. "I'm Constance Schultz. The bishop is my husband. This is my friend, Dinah Lapp. Her husband is our minister and a great help to the bishop."

"I'm pleased to meet you. I'm Maisie Schrock, Nathan's sister-in-law. His late wife was my sister, Annie."

"We heard of the tragedy only a few days ago. Accept our condolences," Dinah said. "We have come to see what we can do to help."

Maisie was moved by the sincerity and sympathy in their eyes. The Amish rallied around one another during times of trial.

"*Danki.* It's been difficult for me. Annie was my twin."

"*Gott* allowed it," Constance said softly. "We cannot understand His ways. We can only accept them."

"I know, and I pray for acceptance." She blinked back her tears. "Come and meet my nephew and niece. This is Jacob and Charity." She led the way to the sofa.

Both women bent over the baskets and cooed with delight. Constance looked at Maisie. "The little girl has such red hair. Does she have a temper to go with it?"

"Not that I have seen yet. I pray she doesn't develop one." Maisie patted her own head. "It can be a burden."

Dinah laughed. "You must meet my daughter-in-law, Gemma. She's a redhead, too."

"Would you like some *kaffi*? It won't take but a minute to put it on."

"Sounds *wunderbar*," Dinah said.

Happy to have such pleasant company, Maisie bustled around the kitchen fixing coffee and putting slices of her fresh bread and the leftover spread Nathan had made on the table.

Constance gathered up the material Maisie had cut out and moved it to one side. "I see you're getting some sewing done."

"Nathan doesn't have any clothes for them except what few things my sister had and what the hospital could send home with him."

"Do you have children of your own?" Dinah asked.

Maisie sat at the table while she waited for the coffee to perk. "I don't. My husband passed away some time ago. We were not blessed with children."

"That must make your sister's children especially precious to you, then," Constance said.

"It does. They are the only family I have left." Maisie felt the tears well up in her eyes.

She found herself telling the women everything about her life in Missouri, her trip to Maine, learning of her sister's death and arriving unannounced on Nathan's doorstep. She left out the part about Annie leaving Nathan. She didn't think he would want that to become common knowledge and neither did she. It didn't reflect well on Annie.

Constance leaned across the table and patted Maisie's hand. "Nathan is fortunate to have you here to care for his new babies."

"He finds my presence distressing."

"Why?" Dinah asked.

"Because Annie and I are—were—identical twins. He sees the woman he loved and lost every time he looks at me. He doesn't want me here."

"No twins are ever exactly the same," Constance said. "Surely he could tell you apart before she died."

"We didn't see much of each other before he moved here. Nathan was new to our community. He met and married my sister very quickly. I was busy taking care of my father during his illness and running our farm after my husband died. I reckon Nathan seldom saw us side by side."

"He'll soon see that you are different from your sister," Dinah said in an encouraging tone as she took another slice of bread.

Constance leaned back and folded her arms across her chest. "Is that why he asked my husband to see if anyone in the community wanted a job as a *kinder heeda*?"

"Nathan wants me to go back to Missouri."

"And what do you want to do?" Constance asked gently.

"I want to care for my sister's children. But if their father won't let me, I don't see how I can make him."

"That's true." Constance rubbed her chin. "Perhaps my husband should have a word with him."

"Nathan isn't a member of our congregation," Dinah reminded her. "Your husband's well-meaning words may not carry much weight."

"It's a family matter," Maisie said quickly. "I'd rather you left it between Nathan and myself." He wouldn't appreciate her involving the bishop. He was a man who liked to solve his own problems.

Constance nodded. "I understand. If the Lord wants you to stay in Maine, He will show you the path. Now, would you like to see what we brought?" she asked brightly.

Puzzled, Maisie rose and followed them to the door. Outside she saw their open buggy was packed with boxes, quilts and even furniture. There were two cradles and a rocking chair.

Maisie opened one of the cardboard boxes and pulled out a little sleeper. It was used but in wonderful condition. It was too big for the babies now, but in a few months it would be perfect. "This is very generous." She hugged the two women.

"If things don't work out between you and Nathan, come see me," Constance said. "There is always a place at our table for as long as you want. Now, let's get these things inside. It looks like rain."

For the first time since leaving Missouri, Maisie felt truly welcomed. She realized she wouldn't have to leave when Nathan found someone to care for the babies. With the help of friends like Constance and Dinah, she could make a life here in Maine and stay close to her sister's children.

Nathan was greeted by the sight of an unfamiliar open buggy parked in front of his cabin when he returned home. The brown-and-white pony hitched to it looked up and whinnied to Sassy. She ignored him as she headed for the barn.

Nathan unhitched the buggy and pulled off her harness before leading the mare into his corral. He rubbed her down and walked her to make sure she was cooled off before he let her drink. Giving her a final pat on her shoulder, he closed the corral gate. Sassy went to the middle of the enclosure, put her nose to the ground and turned in a tight circle before lying down and enjoying a roll in the grass.

Women's voices and laughter spilled out the door as Nathan approached. He stopped in the doorway until one of the women noticed he was there.

"You must be Nathan Weaver." An Amish woman with wire-rimmed spectacles smiled at him from his kitchen. She was holding his naked daughter. Maisie wrapped a towel around the babe and took her in her arms.

"You've just missed bathing the babies," the second woman said as she sat holding Jacob on the sofa. There was a large pile of infant clothing and quilts beside her. "Charity spit up all over herself and her brother."

Maisie kissed Charity's cheek. "Mmm, clean babies smell so sweet."

She nodded toward the woman with glasses.

"Nathan, this is Constance Schultz, the bishop's wife, and that is Dinah Lapp. Her husband is one of the ministers. Sisters, this is my brother-in-law, Nathan Weaver."

Dinah got to her feet and laid the baby in a wooden cradle Nathan had never seen before. A second one sat beside it. She turned to face him. "God's ways are beyond our comprehension, but His love and mercy will comfort you in your time of grief."

He didn't reply. There was no comfort for him, only unanswered questions.

"We were just getting ready to leave," the bishop's wife said. "I'm glad we had the opportunity to meet you. My husband is seeking someone to take care of the children for you. He hasn't found anyone yet, but he's still looking. In the meantime you are blessed to have your wife's sister caring for them. It's easy to see how much she loves them."

"I'll walk you out," Maisie said.

"I'll bring my sewing machine by this weekend," Constance said.

Maisie bit the corner of her lip. "All right, if you're sure you don't need it for a few days."

"If I do I know where it will be," Constance said with a chuckle.

Maisie handed Charity to Nathan and followed her guests out the door. He saw the women hug each other before they got in their buggy. He couldn't hear what they were saying, but Maisie nodded. She smiled and waved as the women drove away.

When she came back inside, she was still smiling.

"What were they doing here?" he asked.

"They stopped in to see how we are getting along and to bring us some things they thought we could use. They brought baby clothes and baby blankets. Even a pair of quilts for us."

She gestured toward the kitchen counter. "And they brought all that food. Freshly canned vegetables and fruit from their gardens. A ten-pound bag of flour and sugar for baking. There is even a moose-meat casserole ready to go into the oven for our supper tonight. They tell me that propane appliances are permitted in this church district, so they are able to keep meat frozen in a freezer. They also said to tell you that you are welcome to store your meat with them when you go hunting this fall."

"I didn't ask for any of this. I can provide for my family. I don't need the charity of others."

She frowned at him. "They didn't come to offer charity."

He gestured with one hand around the cabin. "Then what would you call this? Food. Clothing. Cradles for the babies and a rocking chair."

He pointed to the corner by the fireplace, where he had just noticed the new piece of furniture.

Maisie folded her arms. "I call it a gesture of friendship extended to a new member of their community. Isn't that what we Amish do? We care for one another. We don't wait for someone to ask for help. We just give it. Isn't that the way you want your children to behave when they grow up? How will they learn about generosity and kindness unless they see it firsthand?"

"It's my job to teach them."

Maisie shook her head sadly. "Oh, Nathan. This is about more than your feelings of being a poor provider. We all need help sometimes. We must give it and receive it in equal measure. This is about being part of a community who live and worship together to please *Gott*. If you aren't a part of that then you aren't truly Amish and your children won't be, either."

How did Maisie find the core of his inner fears so easily? He hadn't been an adequate provider. He had failed Annie and he was failing his son and daughter.

He looked away. "What did you tell them about Annie? Will everyone know that she left me?" Shame burned like acid in the back of his throat.

"I told them that my sister was traveling

to be with you when she went into labor and had to go to a hospital. She died before you or I could be with her. Nothing else needs to be said. I don't wish to besmirch my sister's reputation. She repented, and she was making amends. I'm thinking of the children and what they'll hear about her when they're growing up."

"That she took off and left me two months after our wedding with only a note that said she thought she could live Amish but she couldn't anymore?"

"They will never hear that from me. Their mother was on her way to be with their father in his new home in Maine, but *Gott* took her to heaven instead."

"You make it sound like her actions were nothing more than a trip to town. It was months of worry and wondering and never finding peace even when I prayed. Every day I waited for the mail, hoping she would send me a letter, a card, something. Do you know what that's like?"

She stepped close and laid her hand on his arm. "I do, Nathan. I prayed for the same things. I waited and bore my disappointments and cried my tears in secret, but I never hardened my heart against her. I loved her, too."

He gazed into Maisie's eyes. They sparkled

with unshed tears for the grief and pain they had both endured.

Then he noticed something else about her eyes. They were green like Annie's, but Maisie had flecks of gold in hers that Annie hadn't had.

She wiped away the moisture with both hands. "I need to tell you something else, Nathan. I'm not saying this to make you angry. I'm not leaving New Covenant."

"Are we back to this again? I decide who takes care of my children."

Her face grew stoic. "That is your right," she said in a clipped tone.

"I'm not going to change my mind." He wanted to shout, but he kept his voice deliberately even.

She folded her hands demurely in front of her. "If you don't want me to be their *kinder heeda*, I must be content to be the aunt who lives down the road. I will find employment and see them as often as I can. I will bake birthday cakes and make cookies when they come to visit. I'll see them at church."

She raised her chin. "I don't care how many bus tickets you buy for me. I'm not going anywhere."

He leaned close. "We'll see about that."

Chapter Six

Maisie saw a muscle twitch in Nathan's clenched jaw. He was angry, but what could he do? She was a grown woman. He had no control over her life.

Of course, he could order her out of his house right now. She swallowed hard. He wouldn't, would he? He stared at her so long her resolve began to waver.

"You may live wherever you like," he snapped. "But it won't be here any longer than necessary."

She let out the breath she'd been holding. "I understand. If you would like your loft back I will gladly sleep in the barn."

It took a minute, but he finally shook his head. "That won't be necessary."

"*Goot.* I'll call you when supper is ready. I need to put away the things our friends have brought us."

"Your friends," he snapped, staring at his feet.

Her heart went out to him. He was so alone. There was a wall around him that he refused to let people inside. "They will be your friends, too, Nathan. Maybe not today, but when you're ready to be part of a community again."

He looked up with a perplexed expression. "How do you do that?"

She tipped her head slightly. "Do what?"

"Know what I'm feeling."

"Did you forget that I lost my husband? After John's death, making any choice was hard. I only wanted to be left alone to grieve. I avoided people. I thought I should be stronger. I didn't want others to see how broken I was. In time that passed. I found purpose in taking care of my father during his illness. I opened myself up to people again and realized that I didn't have to be strong all by myself. There were friends who wanted to help ease my way."

"I haven't made friends in this Amish community because I am ashamed of what drove me here. Being alone is nothing new for me. Annie's death didn't change that."

"Only you aren't alone anymore. You have two wonderful children who will make friends of their own someday, go to school, attend church, get into trouble, cause no end of worry for you and weave themselves into the fabric of our Amish way of life."

"I only took my baptismal vows so that I could marry your sister."

She smiled softly. "A lot of young men decide to join the faith for that reason. You need to discover what *Gott* wants from you, Nathan. He has a plan for us all if we open our hearts to it."

"You have an answer for everything."

Maisie stared at the floor. "I don't really." Then she glanced up. "Give yourself some time. It hasn't even been two weeks since you lost Annie."

His expression hardened. "You're wrong about that. I may have buried her last week, but I lost my wife months ago."

He stomped out of the cabin. Maisie watched as he picked up an axe and hiked into the woods.

She felt better that she had told him of her desire to stay in New Covenant, but their relationship hadn't improved with the telling. She grasped the ribbon of her *kapp* and wound it around her finger. There had to be a way to help him overcome the bitterness that hung like a dense fog between them. She liked Nathan in spite of his reluctance to allow her into his life. Under his gruff exterior was a good man. She was sure of it.

Perhaps what she needed to do was smother him with kindness. The trick would be keeping her temper under control in the face of his stubbornness.

Nathan swung the axe with as much force as he could muster. Wood chips flew from the pine he was cutting down. *Whack, whack, whack.*

His chain saw would have made quick work of this tree, but the rhythm of his swing and the bite of the axe soothed him. Finally, the tree came crashing down. He leaned on the axe's handle, breathing heavily. One down, three more to go.

He looked in the direction of the cabin. Maisie wasn't leaving. He would have to accept her occasional presence in his life. She had a right to see her sister's children. He couldn't deny her that. She was as alone in the world as he was. He didn't want to feel sorry for her, yet he did.

He hefted his axe and walked to the next tree he had marked. He picked the spot where he wanted it to fall and started swinging again. These trees would cure over the winter and by next summer they would be ready to be peeled and stacked. They would be used to expand his icehouse.

The tree toppled over within a few feet of where he wanted it. The satisfaction eased his foul mood. He needed a way to deal with Annie's sister just as efficiently. His current method of storming out meant he was getting more work on the farm done, but it also served to cut down the time he spent with his children. He'd be going back to work soon and that meant ten hours away from them each day. As much as he disliked being in the same room with Maisie, he would have to be in the cabin with her in order to see his babies. It didn't sit well, but he had little choice. He'd put up with Maisie's discomforting presence for the children.

Being around the woman was unsettling because she was a reminder of Annie, and because she was too perceptive, as well. When she looked at him with her green-gold eyes she saw things he wasn't ready to face.

He sighed heavily. Maisie was in his life, like it or not. Until he found a full-time nanny for the babies he was simply going to have to make the best of it.

He took down the last two trees he had marked and then headed back toward the cabin.

As soon as he came in, he noticed Maisie had cleared out the boxes. She had everything put away except for the jars of produce that still filled the countertop. She was sitting in the rocker by the fireplace feeding one of the babies. He stepped closer to see which one it was. She held Jacob.

Charity was in the cradle beside Maisie's chair. She was squirming a little but not crying. "Has Charity had her bottle?" he asked.

"Not yet. It's warming in the sink. Jacob was the more impatient of the two. Takes after his father."

He didn't smile. "Maybe so."

"That must mean Charity will take after her mother," Maisie suggested.

That was a chilling thought. "I hope not."

He saw a flash of disapproval in Maisie's eyes, but she didn't say anything. He went to the sink and washed up. After drying his hands, he took the bottle from the pan of warm water, sprinkled some of the formula on his wrist to check the temperature, as the nurse at the hospital had taught him, and then scooped up his daughter. He offered the bottle to Charity. She latched on immediately and began to suckle.

He walked to the sofa and sat down with her.

This was so much different than his first attempts to feed them. Would he and the babies have settled in comfortably without Maisie's arrival? Maybe.

No, of course they would have. He would have figured it out.

"Here." Maisie offered him a burp rag. "It will save your shirt from another milk bath."

"*Danki*, but milk might be an improvement." He picked a few wood chips from his sleeve. "I saw the clothesline, but not a washing machine. Do you launder everything by hand?"

"The washer is in the lean-to next to the barn. I lived in the barn when I first came here. I haven't moved the machine up to the house yet."

"You don't have to do that on my account. I don't want to put you to any trouble."

It was too late for that. "It makes sense to have it here. I'll move it to the back porch tomorrow."

"I heard you chopping down trees. Are you building something new or gathering firewood?"

"Something new for next year. The trees have to dry out and cure before I can use them."

"Are you planning an addition to the cabin?"

"I'm expanding my icehouse. I'll add on to

the cabin in a few years when the *kinder* are old enough to need their own room."

She glanced around. "Where would you put it?"

"Going through the wall behind the kitchen would be the easiest. That way I could add a stove to their room and use the same vent pipe."

"That's clever."

Did she really think so? "I have other ideas for the place."

"Like what?"

"I need to expand the garden and put in a root cellar."

She smiled. "That's why I couldn't find one to store those jars in. I looked everywhere."

He grimaced. "I'm not much of a cook. I usually eat my meals at the canteen on the job site. I haven't canned any vegetables so my garden isn't big. I figure I can pay someone to preserve my produce next summer or barter fresh for canned."

"A well-stocked cellar makes keeping food on the table a lot easier." She put Jacob to her shoulder to burp him.

Nathan did the same to Charity. "At least I don't have to worry about keeping a roof over their heads. Davis pays a good wage. My potato crop will bring in extra money as long as the weather and the market cooperate. That plus my salary should see us through the winter. The hospital won't get all their money right away, but they will be paid."

Maisie swaddled Jacob and laid him in his new cradle. She gave a slight push to start it rocking and then when to the kitchen. "Are you ready to eat?"

He smiled at his little girl. "As soon as she is finished."

"I'll put it on the table. I've never had moose meat before. Have you?"

"I've had it as a summer sausage. It isn't bad."

She wrinkled her nose. "Let's hope it isn't bad in this casserole. I don't care for gamey meat."

"Annie was a picky eater, too." He assumed because Maisie was identical to Annie that she would share the same traits, but Annie never had a temper.

"I'm not as bad as my sister was but there are things I won't eat. Okra for one."

"There's none in my vegetable patch."

"I noticed when I was poking around."

He put Charity's empty bottle on the arm of the sofa and carried her to her cradle. After laying her down, he gave the cradle a gentle push. It began swinging to and fro. "Who donated the baby beds to us?"

"The bishop's brother and his wife. They have twins who are grown but not married, so no grandchildren yet to hand them on to."

"They're well-made."

"According to Constance the bishop's brother is a furniture maker. He's starting his own sawmill."

"A useful business." Nathan rubbed his short beard. "I have some hardwoods in my forest. Maybe I can sell them to him."

"You can talk to him at the service next week."

He looked at her sharply. "You assume that I'm going."

She paused in setting the table. "Of course. I'll be going. Everyone will want to meet the babies. Why would you stay home?"

"I don't want strangers staring at me and wondering what my story is."

Setting the plate down, she turned toward him. "Wouldn't the best way to avoid that be to meet the people and tell them what you want them to know? After that you'll be old news."

He hated to admit that she had a point. "We'll see."

"Goot." She smiled brightly. "When that

was my *daed*'s answer, it always meant he was going to do whatever *Mamm* had asked."

"From me it means we'll see." If she was trying to manipulate him with a pleasant smile she would find it hard going.

"As you say. I'll make sure your suit is washed and pressed just in case you decide to join us. Supper is ready."

The casserole wasn't the best he'd ever eaten but he did take a second helping. Maisie's biscuits were light and fluffy, a far cry from the bricks he knew how to make. When she brought out a plate of brownies for dessert, he happily helped himself to two.

"*Goot* supper," he said, leaning back in his chair after finishing a cup of cocoa.

"I'm happy to see you enjoying it. I was worried you'd starve rather than eat in my company."

"I worked up an appetite cutting trees this afternoon." He hesitated then said, "You remind me of things I want to forget, Maisie. I know that isn't your intent, but it can't be helped. You are so like her."

"What if Charity grows up to resemble Annie? How will you treat her? Will she be punished for her mother's sins because they look alike, too?"

"I'm not punishing you for your sister's transgressions."

"It feels like it to me."

He hadn't considered how she saw his actions. He remained silent. She cleared the table, washed the dishes and wiped down the kitchen before taking up her sewing. She sat in the rocker ignoring him. He stayed at the table, turning his cup around and around in his hands as he thought about what he should say.

"I'm sorry you feel that way, Maisie."

She plopped the little gown she was hemming onto her lap. "I'm a grown woman. I'll survive. For a child it might not be so easy."

He nodded. "Charity will look like Charity. I'll never treat her with anything but love. I promise."

"I should not have suggested otherwise." She reached over and set Charity's cradle to rocking again.

Nathan brought the wringer washing machine up to the back porch the next day and showed Maisie how to use it. It was powered with a small gasoline engine, like her lawn mower at home. It took her several tugs on the pull cord to get it started, but once it was going it was much easier than washing and rinsing diapers and bedding by hand.

The only water in the cabin was a hand pump at the kitchen sink. The two-piece bathroom used water from a roof cistern. Maisie learned the tub was an old-fashioned galvanized relic that hung on the front porch. It had to be brought in and filled by hand.

She had to heat her wash water on the stove and carry it out back to the machine. Nathan took her place caring for the babies while she caught up on his laundry, too. When she was hanging the clothes on the line she noticed several pairs of his work pants had rips in them.

After she was finished with the laundry, Nathan took off into the woods again. He seemed determined to spend as little time in her company as possible. While it was discouraging, because she couldn't bridge the gap between them, it was actually easier to work in the small cabin without his disturbing presence. She had the babies to herself and could enjoy holding and singing to them without worrying that she was upsetting him.

Later that evening Nathan was going over his farm accounts at the kitchen table while she was mending his laundry. She held up a pair of his pants. "What do you do that makes such ragged cuts in your pant legs?"

He looked at her. "I've caught them on my chain saw a few times."

Her eyebrows shot up. "While your legs were in them?"

"I've never had a serious cut."

She poked four fingers through one long slit. "The Lord has been your protector, then."

He shrugged one shoulder. "That day I did need a few stitches."

How dangerous was his job? Something Mr. Davis had said troubled her. "What is a widow-maker?"

Nathan went back to studying his account book. "Why do you ask?"

"Mr. Davis said the other feller broke his leg when a widow-maker came down. What did he mean?"

"A widow-maker is a toppled tree or big limb that is hung up or wedged against another tree. A little bit of wind can bring it down or it can stay wedged for years. You always have to be careful around them. Cutting down the tree they're leaning against can be tricky. You're never sure which way they'll fall."

"I see. Does it happen often that someone gets hurt?"

He glanced her way. "Often enough to make me a very cautious man."

She wiggled her fingers through his slit pants again. "Not cautious enough."

The idea of him being seriously hurt chilled

her to the bone. She had faith in God's mercy, but she also knew how easily life could be snuffed out. One minute her husband, John, had been loading bales of hay into their loft. The next minute, he was lying on the ground with a broken neck. She shuddered at the memory.

The Lord gave, and the Lord hath taken away; blessed be the name of the Lord.

She was relieved when Jacob started fussing. She put her mending aside and picked him up. Holding him close, she rocked him until her painful memories faded. The Lord had taken her husband, her father and her sister, but he had given her two beautiful babies to love.

"Shall I fix him a bottle?" Nathan asked.

"I don't think he's hungry. I think he just wants to be held."

"You take good care of them. I'm grateful. I'll hold him so you can get on with your work."

She didn't want to give up Jacob, but she could see Nathan wanted to hold his son as much as she did, maybe more. She managed a smile. "*Danki*, that would be nice. I'll even give you the rocker."

She rose and transferred the baby into Nathan's arms. He gazed at his son so tenderly it brought a lump to her throat. She was close enough to catch his scent. Sweat, wood smoke, fresh pine sawdust, the saddle soap he had used to clean Sassy's harness that evening—a day's work all layered on top of his own unique smell. She felt her pulse jump and beat faster as a flush crept up her neck.

She stepped back quickly. Her gaze flew to his face. Had he noticed? He was staring at her with a puzzled expression. "Are you okay?"

"I'm fine. I need to get the rest of the clothes off the line." She stumbled back another step then hurried outside. On the back porch she took a deep breath and leaned against the cabin wall until her racing heart slowed.

There was no mistaking her reaction to Nathan. As much as she wanted to deny it, she couldn't. She found him attractive, much more than she should have.

She knew what a passing fancy was. This was not something as simple as that.

How could it have happened without her knowing it? She thought back over their conversations and realized it had started the first night she arrived.

When they stood together in the darkness out by the corral—she had sensed a connection with him then. She thought it was because of their shared grief. Or rather, she wanted to believe that was the reason she felt close to him. Her mind had refused to acknowledge anything else. Until tonight.

He was her sister's husband. A man who couldn't look at her without seeing her sister's betrayal. It would be foolish of her to think he might someday care for her. He would pity her or, worse, laugh at the idea.

He had agreed she might see the children even if she couldn't be their caregiver. She didn't want to jeopardize that.

No, Nathan must never learn how she felt. Now that she recognized what was happening, she would guard her heart and not give this emotion room to grow.

She took a deep breath and went back in the house determined to act as if nothing had changed. Because it hadn't. He didn't want her here.

Keeping her wayward heart in check was harder than Maisie had imagined it would be. She tossed and turned that night long after she heard Nathan leave the cabin. It was hopeless to care so much for him. He would never return those feelings.

At least he was beginning to see her usefulness. He had thanked her for the care she gave the children. That was what she really wanted. To take care of the babies and love them as her own. If Nathan allowed that and nothing else, she would be content.

She bit her lower lip. Would she? Or was she lying to herself?

Chapter Seven

Saturday morning Maisie came down the stairs determined to ignore her irrational attraction to Nathan and concentrate on providing the best possible care to him and his children. Both infants had slept for almost five hours before getting her up to feed them. They were awake again now. Jacob was making his wants known with a loud cry. Charity was making little whimpering noises. She was more patient than her brother.

"I'm coming, Jacob. Don't holler the house down." She started into the kitchen and almost ran into Nathan coming in the back door. Her foolish heart gave a happy leap at the sight of his face. She quickly scooted around him, making sure they didn't touch.

"How are you this morning?" he asked.

"I'm fine."

"You seemed on edge last night."

It would never do for him to notice how he affected her.

"I do get cranky when I'm short of sleep." She glanced at his face. Did he believe her?

He seemed to relax. "I thought that might be the case. I will take care of the babies tonight so you can catch up on some rest."

She opened the can of concentrated formula and added the recommended amount of water from the kettle she kept warming on the back of the stove. "That is not necessary."

"I've abused your generosity. They are my son and daughter. I want to do it. If Jacob's bottle is ready, I'll feed him first since he is so loud."

"I haven't changed him yet."

"I'm not afraid of a dirty diaper or two." To prove his point he went to take care of that chore while she finished mixing the formula. She was pouring the formula into Charity's bottle when Nathan came up beside her to wash his hands at the sink. His shoulder brushed against hers. Her hand shook so badly that she splashed formula down the front of her dress.

He looked at her with a slight frown on his face. "Are you sure you're okay?"

"Don't worry. My clumsiness is not contagious," she said, sounding more annoyed than she intended.

He scowled at her. "I'm sorry I asked."

She screwed the nipple on top of the bottle. "I'm the one who is sorry. Forgive me."

He reached around her for the towel on the counter. She could smell the minty scent of his shaving cream. She closed her eyes and stopped breathing.

"There's nothing to forgive," he said as he took the bottle from her hands and went to feed his son.

Maisie turned to stare out the kitchen window. How long could she keep up the pretense that his closeness didn't affect her?

Charity began to cry in earnest. Maisie glanced over her shoulder. Nathan sat on the sofa with his boy in his arms while he rocked Charity's cradle with his foot to soothe her.

Maisie would keep her foolish heart in check for as long as the babies needed her. Because she needed them, too. She needed someone to love, and to be loved by in return. She was tired of being alone, first with her emotionally distant husband and then with her dying father, who'd constantly asked for Annie instead of the daughter who had cared for him for over a year.

Maisie straightened her shoulders and finished fixing Charity's bottle. She needed to be needed and wanted. Nathan might want her gone, but she wasn't leaving.

She lifted the baby from her cradle and settled into the rocking chair with her. Charity gazed up at her with wide baby-blue eyes.

"Guder mariye, mie lieb," Maisie whispered and kissed her forehead. "Every morning is a *goot* morning when I have you in my arms."

"They make our troubles seem insignificant, don't they?" Nathan was gazing at his son with an expression of undisguised love on his face. Maisie's heart expanded with happiness for him.

"They do," she answered. Annie had carelessly thrown away the love of this man. Maisie had only pity for her sister. She had made poor choices.

Nathan looked up and met Maisie's eyes. Something passed between them at that moment. A shared love, not for one another, but for the children God had so graciously given into their care.

She saw his gaze slide away from her as his mouth tensed. "Annie could have been happy with me and these babies if she hadn't left. We could have had a good life in Missouri."

Maisie's heart ached for the pain he was

sharing. "I think you're right. I don't believe she knew what she was giving up."

"You don't think she knew she was pregnant when she left me?"

Could her sister have been so cruel as to take away a man's children and leave him never knowing they existed? "I can't believe that she did."

"But she had to know within a month or two. Yet she didn't come back. Was there another man she wanted to be their father?"

"You are asking questions without answers, Nathan. Let it be enough that she decided to bring them to you in the end. She has gone to stand before *Gott* and answer for her life. Only He knows her heart. Only He can judge her."

Nathan drew one finger along his son's cheek. "My boy will have questions one day about why he doesn't have a mother. I don't know how I will answer him."

"You will find the words when the time comes. Until then, enjoy these amazing moments. Your children will be grown before you know it. You will never get these days back, Nathan."

"I do enjoy them." He put aside Jacob's empty bottle and raised the babe to his shoulder. He softly patted the boy's back and rested his cheek on the baby's head. Jacob drifted off to sleep, but Nathan didn't put him down. Maisie finished feeding Charity, put her back in her cradle, then slipped out of the cabin, leaving Nathan alone with his children.

She hiked to the top of the rise behind the cabin to her sister's final resting place. She sat in the soft grass beside the grave, drew her knees up to her chin and wrapped her arms around her legs. "You left so much bitterness behind, Annie, but your babies are beautiful. Charity looks like us. Happily, she has your temperament and not mine. Jacob is going to be enough to handle without adding another hothead to the mix."

Maisie plucked a few weeds that had sprouted in the freshly turned earth. "Nathan is such a good man. He's trying to be a good father. I don't understand why you left him."

She groped for answers where there weren't any. "Was it because you knew my marriage to John wasn't a happy one? Were you afraid that you and Nathan would grow apart and come to resent each other?"

Maisie thought back over the conversations she had with her sister about her unhappy marriage and wished she had kept those feelings to herself. Was that why Annie hadn't confided in her, because she wanted to spare Maisie her unhappiness?

"I never resented John. I don't believe he resented me. We had known each other forever. Getting married seemed the thing to do. I thought our love would grow over time. I was wrong. I did care for him. I think he cared for me in his way, but he never could express that. It's a sad way to live, always wishing something would spark that love into being. Forever waiting to hear words you know will never be spoken. Children might have saved us, but I will never know, will I?"

Maisie got to her feet and brushed off her dress. "I hope you are at peace, sister. I pray you can rest easy knowing how much Nathan loves those children. Thank you for bringing them to him."

Maisie glanced around at the meadow and saw wildflowers growing near the edge of the woods. She went over and gathered an armful. Then she laid them gently on Annie's grave. "I will try to help him forgive you, for I know that's what he needs to do."

Nathan stepped outside of his room the next morning and stared at the cabin. As usual, the front door was open and he heard the sound of singing. Maisie was always humming or singing. It was the Amish off Sunday. There wouldn't be prayer services for her to attend. They were held every other week.

He glanced longingly at the forest. Only essential work was allowed on any Sunday. He might not be a member of the local church group, but he abided by the rules of his faith. His tree cutting would have to wait. He sighed heavily and started toward the house. There was a full day ahead of him that he would have to spend with Annie's sister.

He entered the cabin to see her playing with his cat. She was teasing him with a small ball of yarn. The cat would dart out from under the sofa, pounce on it and then scurry back under the furniture. Maisie would laugh and start humming as she pulled the yarn ball closer to the sofa again.

It was like hearing Annie's laugh. He shoved his hands in his pockets. "Morning."

Her smile faded. "*Guder mariye*, Nathan. Your breakfast is in the oven. I didn't know what time you would be in."

He headed for the kitchen. "When my chores are done."

She stayed silent while he ate and cleaned up quickly after he was done. She sat down with his copy of the *Martyrs Mirror* and started reading. The book contained stories of the men and women who had been martyred for their

Anabaptist beliefs. They were the founders of the Amish faith.

He paced the room not knowing what to do. The babies were both quiet. He finally settled in his chair by the fireplace.

Maisie cleared her throat. "My father used to read to us on the off Sundays and in the evenings. It's a fond memory I have of him. Why don't you read to the children now?"

"Aren't they too small to care?"

"Who can say? We are born with open ears. *Gott* must want us to use them."

Nathan shrugged, got up and took his Bible down from the fireplace mantel. Maisie must have dusted it when she was cleaning because the black leather cover was shiny as new.

He carried it back to the table, moved a lamp closer and opened the cover. "What shall I read?"

"Daniel in the lions' den," she said without hesitation and picked up her yarn.

The hint wasn't subtle. "Are sure you don't mean Maisie in the lions' den?"

"Don't be silly. There is no story of Maisie in the Bible."

It had been a while since he had last opened this book. He leafed through the pages until he found the book of Daniel and began to read. When he was finished with the story, he looked over to see her smiling tenderly at Jacob. She glanced at Nathan. "His eyes are open. I think he likes the sound of your voice. Read something else."

"What would you like?"

"The Book of Job."

He turned to those chapters and started reading about Job, his suffering and his unwavering faith in God. Nathan suspected Maisie had chosen that part of the Old Testament to help him see that he was not alone in being tested. Unlike Job, Nathan's faith had wavered.

He glanced at Maisie. She had kept her faith in the face of her own painful losses. She had lost her mother when she was young, her husband when she was little more than a bride, her father and then her only sister without questioning God's plan or doubting His mercy. It was sobering to realize how strong she was. Jacob started stirring. Maisie got up to tend to him.

"Will anyone be visiting today?" Maisie asked after tucking the babies into their cradles later that day.

"I'm not expecting anyone. Why?"

She looked at him in surprise "It's the off Sunday."

"So?"

"It's a day that people normally go visit each other, families, friends. In Missouri we were always going to someone's house or expecting company on our off Sundays."

"I don't like visiting. No one comes here."

Maisie just shook her head. "I don't wonder why."

He finally looked up from the magazine he had decided to read. "What's that supposed to mean?"

"You aren't friendly with your Amish neighbors, Nathan."

"I don't have neighbors. That's why I live up here."

"Lilly Arnett is your neighbor. You said so yourself."

He turned the page of his magazine. "She isn't Amish."

"Well, who is the closest Amish family?"

"The Fishers, I reckon. They live a mile beyond Lilly's place."

"And have you been to visit them?"

"I purchased my harnesses there. Otherwise, I've never had a reason to."

"Have you been to visit the bishop and his wife? Constance is a lovely woman. I'm sure she would enjoy a visit today. I know she'd like to see the twins."

He turned another page. "It's my day of rest."

"I see. I believe I will bake a cake."

His expression brightened. "I like cake."

"I thought that might be the case." She spent the next ten minutes getting a chocolate sheet cake into the oven. Then she washed her hands and went upstairs. When she came down twenty minutes later, she had her Sunday dress on and her traveling bonnet in her hand. She checked on her cake and took it out of the oven. She began to pack some things for the babies and then moved them from their cradles into their carriers.

Nathan gave her a puzzled look. "What are you doing?"

"You may not like to go visiting, but I do. Constance Schultz was kind enough to loan me her sewing machine so I'm taking a cake to her home as a thank-you."

"I thought you were making the cake for me?"

"If there is any left, I will bring some home. Would you please hitch up the buggy?"

"It's my day of rest."

She merely arched one eyebrow and stood waiting. He threw down his magazine and got out of his chair. "If you're going to nag, I might as well get it over with. I'll enjoy my peace and quiet while you're gone."

"I'm sure you will. I'll enjoy chocolate cake and *kaffi* with my new friends."

He grumbled when he went out the door, but she couldn't hear what he was saying. She bent down to pick up the babies. "He might sound like an old bear sometimes but your *daed* is a fine fellow at heart."

She was waiting on the porch with the babies' carriers over each arm and the cake in a cardboard box by her feet when he led Sassy up to the steps. Maisie went around to the driver's side and got in without waiting for his help. She smiled at him out the open side. "Would you fetch the cake for me, Nathan? It's in that box on the porch."

He rolled his eyes but did as she asked. She put the cake on the other side of the babies. "I don't know how long I'll be."

"Be back before dark," he said sternly.

"Of course." She smiled at him and picked up the lines. "I left a piece of cake for you on the table. Sassy, walk on." The horse took off at a leisurely pace.

Nathan walked back into the cabin and stood with his hands in his pockets. The quiet emptiness was almost unnerving. Maisie was always humming softly or talking to the babies when she wasn't clattering pans or dishes in the kitchen or sweeping the floor. She was never rushed, never impatient—she simply went about her work.

She didn't jabber at him the way Annie used to in a giggling, immature way that he'd found cute, but he was always aware of Maisie. It shouldn't be that way.

He sat down in his chair and picked up his magazine but didn't open it. He stared into space and wondered if he should've gone with her. What if the babies became fussy? Would she concentrate on her driving or try to tend to them? The road out this way was narrow. It didn't get much traffic, but it only took a moment of inattention to end up in the ditch.

He looked at Buddy, who was gazing mournfully at the front door. "I'm not going to worry about them. I don't want you to worry about them, either. She's not going to give you or me a second thought. She has the babies with her, and she will be happily showing them off to everyone."

He opened his magazine and started reading until he realized it was an article he had already finished. He laid it aside and drummed his fingers on the arm of the chair.

They were his children. If anyone was going to act the happy new parent, it should be him.

He heard a sound in the kitchen and looked

that way. Buddy had his front feet on the tabletop trying to reach the slice of cake in the center with one paw. His leg wasn't quite long enough. "*Shlecht hund!* Bad dog. Get down."

Nathan crossed the room and picked up the plate. "She left it for me. Not for you. Besides, I hear chocolate is bad for dogs."

He got a fork and sat down at the table to eat his treat. It was moist and delicious. He looked at the dog, who was eyeing him hopefully. "For all Maisie's faults, the woman does know how to cook."

Buddy barked twice.

"What are her faults? I'm glad you asked."

He thought for a long moment but couldn't come up with much. "She has a bit of a temper when she does get riled."

He snapped his fingers and pointed at Buddy. "She irritates me." He twitched his mouth to one side. "I don't think she does it on purpose."

Maisie didn't have many faults other than the fact that she reminded him of Annie every time he looked at her. That wasn't something she could change.

The sooner he found a nanny for the children, the sooner he would have relief from Maisie's disturbing presence. He got up and took his hat from the peg. Maybe there was a message for him. His ad had been in the grocery store for several days. "Come on, Buddy. Let's go check the phone."

Maisie was relieved to find the bishop and his wife were at home. It turned out that she wasn't the only visitor. Michael Shetler and his wife, Bethany, were there along with Dinah Lapp and her husband, Leroy. The bishop and the men were playing horseshoes in the backyard. They left the women to provide refreshments, enjoy catching up on the current news in the community and pass the much-admired babies from arm to arm.

"I heard that Esther Fisher's sister, Julia, is planning to move here in the spring. She wants to open an Amish bakery," Bethany said. She smiled at Charity, who was yawning.

Constance frowned. "But I thought her family owned a bakery in Illinois."

"Her stepmother has convinced Esther's father to sell the business," Bethany said. "They are moving to the Amish community near Sarasota, Florida."

"Our daughter lived there for a while," Dinah said. "She claims it's a beautiful area, but I was thrilled that she decided to return home and marry Jesse." She tucked the blanket under Jacob's chin. "I couldn't bear to have my grandchildren be so far away."

"What about you, Maisie?" Constance asked. "Will you be returning to Missouri?"

"I've decided to stay in Maine."

Constance pressed a hand to her heart. "I'm so glad Nathan is letting you stay. You are the one who should be looking after his babies."

Maisie shook her head. "Nathan still wants someone else to care for the children. He wasn't happy when I told him I'm not leaving, but he has no say in the matter."

"*Goot* for you," Bethany declared.

"If you won't be staying with Nathan, where will you stay?" Dinah asked in a worried tone.

Maisie smiled with more confidence than she was feeling. "I will get a job and find a place of my own. Constance has offered to let me stay with them until I get settled. I will see the babies as often as I can. He will be gone to work in the lumber camp most days, so I don't think it will be a problem if I keep the nanny company."

Dinah took a sip of her coffee and put her cup down. "I'm sure whoever it is will be glad of an extra set of hands. I know I was when Gemma and her brother came along. Babies are wonderful but they can be exhausting."

Constance chuckled. "You are fortunate that

you have twins first. That way you have no idea how much work only one baby can be."

"It's a shame Nathan has to work in the lumber camp," Maisie said softly. "I wish he could spend more time with them. They grow up so fast, and he will miss so much."

She looked up to see all the women staring at her. "What?"

"It sounds like you care for Nathan," Constance said with a strange glint in her eye.

Maisie frowned as she looked from face to face. "Of course I do. He's my brother-in-law. We may not always get along, but he's a fine man and he deserves to be at home with his children as any Amish father would hope to be. Is it wrong to wish that for him?"

"Not at all," Dinah said quickly. "You are to be commended for your concern. I mean, you say he does not want you there, so it would be understandable if you found him objectionable."

"I don't. He was married to my sister and I owe him my respect."

"That's only right. Tell me, do you think he will remarry?" Constance took a sip of her coffee.

Chapter Eight

Maisie sat stunned by the bishop's wife's question. Would Nathan remarry? She hadn't considered it. She looked away from the sharp eyes of her hostess. "It's much too soon for him to think about that."

Constance set her cup down. "Of course. I wasn't suggesting he would rush into anything, but he is going to need a wife to help raise these children. Not soon, but one day. He can't do it alone."

Maisie felt the need to defend him and looked up. "Nathan will manage on his own. He's determined to do so. And I admire him for that."

"We all do," Dinah said, giving Constance a speaking glance.

"Of course," Constance said sincerely. "A man may raise a family without a wife. I've seen it done, but I know from my years of being married that burdens which are shared are cut in half and joys that are shared are more than doubled. I would wish any parent, a man or a woman, to have a spouse to share their life with."

Maisie nodded slowly as the idea sank in. "Nathan and the children deserve to be happy."

"I understand Nathan built his own cabin," Bethany said brightly. Maisie was grateful for the change of subject.

"He did. It's quite beautiful and very functional. I know that there are improvements that could be made, but I see why log homes are so popular."

"Are they?" Constance asked with interest.

"Oh, they are. I noticed a little house on the bishop's lot where he builds sheds. Has he considered selling log homes?"

Constance became thoughtful. "Not that he has ever mentioned to me."

Maisie smiled. "It was just a thought on my part. Nathan has considerable skill as a builder, and I do wonder if it isn't going to waste simply cutting down trees for someone else."

She held her breath, wondering if she had done enough to plant the idea in the mind of the bishop's wife. If Nathan could work for the bishop, he wouldn't need to travel so far to earn a living. He could build the homes on his own property and have the bishop handle the sales.

A sly smile curved Constance's lips. "I'll tell my husband about your idea. You are looking out for Nathan's best interests, aren't you?"

"He has suffered a great deal. I fear his faith may be shaken. I know that I have depended on others when I was questioning. Knowing there are people who care about you can make all the difference during a dark time."

Bethany looked at everyone. "We have all been the recipients of loving-kindness when it mattered most."

The women nodded in agreement. Constance clasped her hands together. "I almost forgot the most important news. There is a new family coming here from upstate New York. They want to farm, and land here is cheaper than in New York, so they are bringing their entire family. They have twelve children."

Bethany laughed. "My grandfather would've been so happy with that news. He prayed that he was doing the right thing when he first came to New Covenant to start an Amish community and invited other Amish families to join him."

"Twelve children." Dinah chuckled. "They

are almost single-handedly going to double our population." Everyone laughed.

Maisie stayed until early evening and then decided it was time to take the children home. Her visit had cemented her desire to remain in New Covenant. She was among friends here. They were already making her feel at home.

Only one thing troubled her about the day. She hadn't considered that Nathan might remarry until Constance asked the question. If he did, the children would become his wife's children and Maisie would have to accept that.

When she drove into the farmyard, she saw Nathan had moved one of the kitchen chairs out to the porch. He was leaning back on two legs against the cabin wall. She thought he looked relieved to see her, but she couldn't be sure. He sat in the shadows.

"I thought I said before dark?"

"It's not dark."

"Hmm. It will be before long."

She got down and lifted the babies out. "The sun won't set for another hour. We are back safe and sound. You needn't have worried."

"When you take my newborns and go wandering around the country I have a right to be concerned, don't I?"

"You are absolutely right. Does that mean you will come with me next time?"

He frowned. "We'll see."

It was a small victory. Maisie held back her grin. "Would you please put Sassy away?"

He took the horse by the bridle and glanced back. "I doubt you even brought a crumb of cake home. The piece you left me wasn't very big."

Maisie gave him her saddest look. "I didn't. Everyone took extra slices. But I did bring home half a cherry pie that Bethany made. Does that help?"

"I like apple better, but cherry pie will work."

She pressed the back of her hand to her brow and tried to sound dramatic. "I'm so glad you approve. I was terribly concerned it wouldn't do. Is food all you think about?"

His expression turned from amused to stoic. "Annie used to do that. Put her hand on her forehead and make a big drama about some little thing."

Maisie's happiness slipped away. "We used to pretend we were acting in a play when we were children."

"She was good at pretending to care. I wonder if you share her talent."

Maisie didn't know how to reply to that. "I'll get supper on."

She took the babies and hurried inside.

* * *

The following morning after breakfast Maisie was packing Nathan's lunch for the day. They hadn't spoken since the previous evening. He was sitting at the table drinking his second cup of coffee when she happened to glance over and saw he was watching her with an odd light in his eyes.

She had to know what he was thinking. "What?"

He stared down at his coffee. "Nothing. You make a good cup of *kaffi*." He took another sip. *"Danki."*

"Annie's coffee was like dishwater. A little color but not much taste."

Maisie chuckled. "That's exactly what John said about my coffee when we were first married. He was the one who taught me to make it this way."

"I wish I could've met him."

Maisie looked at Nathan in surprise. "I wish you could've, too. The two of you were a lot alike."

He leaned back and hooked one arm over the top rung of his chair. "In what ways?"

"He was a thinker, a planner. He didn't like to rush into a project."

"Since you and Annie were so alike I imagine you were at his side telling him how to do it better."

She smiled and looked down. "I did, which annoyed him to no end."

"Don't I know it. I had carefully planned and built a new henhouse. I was almost done with it when Annie came out, put her hands on her hips and said, 'You have the door on the wrong side.'"

"Did you?" Maisie asked, happy to hear Nathan talking about her sister without bitterness in his voice.

"I put the door on the side closest to the barn, where their feed would be stored."

"What did she think was wrong with that?"

"It was on the side farthest away from the house. She would have to walk around to the other side to gather the eggs in the morning. We had a heated discussion about it. It was only twenty extra steps."

"That would've been an easy fix," Maisie said.

"The door was already on. I wasn't about to move it."

"Of course not."

He frowned slightly. "Annie's solution was to put a second door in the henhouse. I suppose that would be your solution, too?"

"Mine would've been much simpler. I would

let you gather the eggs every morning and I wouldn't have had to walk out at all."

He chuckled. "Amazingly simple. It never occurred to me."

"What did you do?"

"I put in a second door to make her happy." His smile faded. "I guess it didn't after all."

Maisie finished packing his lunch and handed him the blue-and-white lunch pail. He took it and looked at her intently. "There was a message on the phone this morning. A woman is coming to interview for the nanny position today at noon. She's Amish. Her name is Agnes Martin."

"Oh. I see." So quickly? Maisie wasn't ready to give up caring for the twins.

"I'll leave it to you to decide if she knows enough about babies. If so, I'll talk to her myself. I think I hear Jimmy's truck coming."

She clutched her hands together to keep from reaching for him. "Be careful out there."

He crossed to the babies and kissed each of them. "Be *goot* for your aunt Maisie."

"That's the only way they know how to be." She wished he didn't have to go. Things seemed better between them this morning.

A vehicle honked outside. Nathan crossed to the door but paused before he opened it. "Make a list of things the *kinder heeda* will need to know. Feeding schedules and stuff. You don't have to take the first woman that shows up. My ad should be in today's paper. Are you going to be all right alone? I mean without me here?"

That he was concerned about her warmed her insides. "Don't worry. I know where the phone shack is. I have Sassy if I need to go somewhere. I have food, formula for the babies, water, warm clothing and Buddy to keep me company. I'll be fine. It's not like you're going to be gone a month."

He gave her a lopsided grin. "That would make you happy, wouldn't it?"

She waited until he was out the door and pressed a hand to her heart. "I'm afraid not, Nathan. I'm going to have enough trouble getting through today."

When she was sure the truck was gone, she went out and brought in the bathtub. She normally sponged off in the tiny bathroom, but if she was going to meet a potential nanny she wanted to be at her best.

Fortunately, between heating water and hauling it out when she was done with her bath, taking care of the babies, making sure the cabin was spotless and working on the storage project she was planning, she had little time to think about Nathan. When she wasn't busy, he was all she thought about. Was he being safe? Was he missing his children? Had he given her a single thought? Would he ever get past thinking that she was like her sister?

Maisie shook her head at her own foolishness. No doubt he was delighted to be back with his lumberjack companions and hadn't given her a second thought except to hope the nanny would be a good fit and Maisie would need to find a new place to live.

When Agnes Martin arrived, Maisie tried to keep an open mind. The woman was in her late fifties or early sixties. She was slender with a pinched face that seemed to be on the verge of a identifying a sour smell.

Maisie welcomed her in. "Would you like some coffee?"

Mrs. Martin untied her bonnet strings as she and Maisie sat down. "I understood that Mr. Weaver would be the one to interview me."

"I'm his sister-in-law. I've been giving Nathan a hand taking care of the babies."

"Then why does he need a nanny?"

"I'm sure Nathan can answer that question better than I can. I do know he wants someone who can take on a permanent position. I've taken the liberty of writing down some of the things you will need to know about Charity and Jacob. Their feeding schedule and such. Would you like to meet them?"

She looked around. "Isn't this a live-in position? I'd like to see my room. This cabin certainly doesn't have much to recommend it."

Maisie realized Nathan hadn't included enough information in his flyers at the grocery store. "Nathan has plans to add on to the cabin, but for now he would like you to come daily, Monday through Friday."

Agnes got to her feet. "Then I have wasted my time. I'm not driving out here to the back of beyond every day."

"I can tell Nathan that you would prefer to watch the children at your house during the day."

"I live with my daughter. I don't believe she would like two squalling infants disturbing the household."

Jacob decided at that moment to give a loud, lusty cry. Maisie hurried to pick him up and quiet him.

Agnes tied the strings of her traveling bonnet. "You should let the child cry. If you don't you are spoiling him into thinking someone will answer his every demand."

Maisie smiled as politely as she could manage. "I appreciate your advice. And I'm sorry you made the trip for nothing. I don't believe it's a position that you would enjoy."

"Tell Mr. Weaver that when he has the additional room added I will reconsider."

Maisie followed the woman to the door. "I'll be sure to pass on that message."

When the door closed behind pinch-faced Agnes, Maisie hugged to Jacob. "I think you had a narrow escape. I will be happy to tell your father we didn't suit her."

Maisie spent the remainder of the day enjoying the babies and holding them as much as she could. When they were both fast asleep, she sat down with her sewing.

At six o'clock she got up and started supper, but couldn't stop watching the clock on the mantel. It was almost seven before she heard the sound of a pickup engine. Although she wanted to rush to the door, she didn't. She took a seat on the couch with some sewing on her lap as if she wasn't on pins and needles waiting for his return.

She waited but he didn't come inside. She heard the sound of the truck leaving, but he still didn't come in. She rose and went to the door. There was no sign of him outside. What on earth was he doing? Didn't he know she had supper waiting for him? It would be his own fault if the meat loaf turned into brown brick.

She shut the door and went back to her sewing. Twice she stabbed herself with the needle because she wasn't paying attention to what she was doing. She was sucking on her smarting finger when she finally heard the door open. She turned to glare at him. "What have you been doing?"

"The chores. The horses needed to be fed. The stalls cleaned. I had to shut up the chickens and the ducks for the night. My farm chores don't vanish because I work at the lumber camp."

Maisie had seldom felt so foolish. Of course, he would do his chores before he came in for the evening. She tried to smile. "How was your day?"

He hung his hat on a wooden peg by the door. His hair was glistening wet. He'd taken the time to wash up before coming in.

"Busy. We're trying to get caught up. I spent a lot of the day repeating the story of Annie's death and my new fatherhood to different people. The *Englisch* are a curious lot. I should have called a meeting first and told everyone at the same time."

"I'm sorry if that was painful."

"After the first telling it wasn't so bad." He crossed the room to squat beside the cradles. "How were *mei kinder*?"

"*Wunderbar*. Both of them. I had them on

quilts on the floor and Jacob almost turned himself over."

Nathan grinned at his boy. "Are you going to be a traveling man, then?"

"Charity is happy to lie on her back and take it all in. Nothing much upsets her. I did have to put Buddy out. He insists on licking their toes when they're on the floor."

"And what does the cat think of them?"

"He ignores them."

He stood up straight and slipped his hands in the pockets of his pants. "How did the interview with Agnes Martin go?"

"She assumed it was a live-in position. She doesn't want to drive out here on a daily basis. I told her there were plans to add on to the cabin in the future and she said to contact her then."

"I didn't plan to do that for at least another year. I didn't realize it might be a problem. Did she seem to like the babies?"

"She didn't actually ask to see them. Jacob started crying and she told me I shouldn't pick him up because it would spoil him."

Nathan frowned. "He's a newborn. Newborns cry."

"I didn't say I agreed with her. I'm merely telling you what she said."

"Then we will cross her off the list."

"You have a list? Have more people applied?"

"Not yet, but they will." Nathan settled himself in his chair and put his head back. "Something smells good."

Maisie gave a little shriek. "My meat loaf. Oh, I hope it's not burnt." She rushed to the stove, pulled the oven door open and took out the pan using the corners of her apron.

"How is it? I can eat burnt," he said.

"The edges are crisp, but it's fine." Buddy had followed her into the kitchen and sat beside her with his tail wagging and his tongue hanging out. He licked his chops hopefully. She shook her head. "There's nothing for you tonight. Go away."

She could've sworn he looked disappointed as he padded to the door. Nathan got up to let him out. "And how was your day?" he asked, looking in her direction.

"Productive. Besides speaking with Agnes Martin, I did some housework and finished two new pants and a shirt for Jacob. They are lying on the back of the couch."

He walked over and held up the shirt. "Don't you think this is too big for him?"

"In another few months it will be too small. I wanted to give him some growing room."

"And this is for Charity?" He picked up a bonnet Maisie had trimmed with tiny pink bows. Would he disapprove? "I know it's a little fancy, but it looks adorable on her. Do you want me to take the bows off?"

"*Nee*, I like them. She is a babe, after all, and doesn't have to dress plain."

"That's what I thought." She smiled at him. It was good to have him home. The cabin felt complete when he was in it.

He laid the bonnet back on the sofa and put his hands in his pockets. "Can we eat now? I'm starving."

"Of course. Sit down. I'll have it ready in a minute."

Maisie knew she was blushing. Nathan wasn't interested in looking at baby clothes or clean floors. He'd been working long hours at a dangerous job. The least she could do was feed him when he came home, even if it was burnt meat loaf.

Nathan finished his meal in silence. It was good to be home. He had missed his children. He had even missed Maisie a little. While it had been good to see the men he worked with again, he'd found it hard to keep his mind on his job. Even one close call with a log that slipped out of its cable wasn't enough to force him to put Maisie out of his mind. Now that she was sitting across the table from him, he tried to figure out why.

Was it because of the things she said and did that reminded him of Annie? Or was it because of the way she showered his babies with love and tried to make his sparse cabin homey? He'd noticed the clean windows and floors, and how the house always smelled like something good was cooking. It had been a long time since Nathan felt at home, even in the place he'd built with his own hands.

He went to the rocking chair and took down his Bible. He caught Maisie giving him a puzzled look.

"I enjoyed reading to them yesterday. I thought I'd read to them while you clean up."

"I think that's a wonderful idea."

When Maisie finished with the supper dishes, she sat in the rocker and began to hem a gown she had made out of a soft yellow material. He caught her yawning several times.

Before Nathan was finished reading the story of David and Goliath, Jacob began to fuss. He knew Charity wouldn't be far behind her brother in demanding her supper.

Maisie put her sewing aside and went to the icebox to get their bottles. Nathan got up and took them from her hands. "I'll do this feeding. You look tired. Why don't you turn in?"

"I can take care of them." She reached for the bottles.

He held them away from her. "I haven't seen them all day. I want to do this."

"All right. If you put it that way. I am tired. I believe I will go to bed. Don't forget to warm the milk."

"I won't. Good night, Annie." He placed the bottles in a bowl and filled it with hot water from the kettle on the stove.

He turned back to see Maisie still standing beside the icebox. "I thought you were going to bed?"

"You called me Annie."

Something in the way she said it held his attention. He had hurt her feelings. "Sorry. I wasn't thinking."

"That's all right. I know how easy it is to confuse us. I saw my reflection in a mirror at the fabric shop last week and I thought Annie was standing in front of me. It's hard to accept she's really gone. Good night, Nathan."

"Good night, Maisie."

"Thanks for feeding them."

"Sure." He watched her climb the stairs with slow, lagging steps. Was she simply tired or was something else weighing on her? It surprised him how much he wanted to know.

Would she confide in him if he asked?

Chapter Nine

Maisie felt like crying as she lay in bed listening to the sound of Nathan's voice. He talked to the babies while he fed them, telling them about his day. His voice was tender and reassuring.

He was a good father. She could imagine him teaching Jacob how to drive a buggy or handle a team. He would build the swing for Charity and push her higher when she begged him to.

She could imagine herself standing off to the side watching, not really a part of the activities. Nathan would be smiling at the children and when he caught sight of her that smile would vanish because for an instant he would see Annie standing there.

Maisie wasn't sure she could endure those mistaken looks. Nathan would glance away. He might even apologize if he knew Maisie had caught the look. In time, it might not happen as often, but Maisie knew her sister's shadow would always be between them.

A tear rolled from the corner of her eye to dampen her pillowcase. For the first time in her life she wished she hadn't been born a twin, at least not an identical one.

Then again, she wouldn't give up any part of her childhood with her dearest friend always at her side. They seldom had to tell each other what they were thinking. Annie always seemed to know. And Maisie had read her sister just as easily. It was why Annie's disappearance had felt like such a betrayal.

Maisie should've known what her sister was thinking. She should have prevented it. Maybe then she could be watching Annie and Nathan playing with their children and standing off to the side wouldn't feel so painful.

But God allowed Annie's death. Maisie accepted that. She had come to help but she was only bringing more pain to Nathan and herself by staying. Was leaving, as he wished, the right thing to do? Maybe it was.

Eventually she fell asleep. When she opened her eyes again she saw the morning sky growing light outside her tiny bedroom window.

She sat up with a start. How could she have

slept through the night without hearing the babies? She grabbed her robe and hurried down the stairs. She stopped on the next-to-last tread. Nathan was sprawled on the couch asleep. There were two empty baby bottles on the floor beside him and the cradles had been pulled up next to him.

Buddy sat up and trotted to the door. He looked back over his shoulder at her. She crossed the floor on bare feet and let the dog out as quietly as she could. When she turned around she saw Nathan was awake and watching her. She self-consciously tightened the belt of her robe. Her hair hung over her shoulder in a long braid that went past her hips. She flipped it behind her.

She stared at her toes. "You should have woke me."

"I realized you hadn't had a full night's sleep in almost a week. I know how that feels."

"I appreciate that, but you can't have gotten much rest."

He sat up and twisted his neck one way, and then the other. "This couch leaves something to be desired."

"I feel awful. I should have heard them fuss. I always do."

"I kept them close to me so I heard their

first peeps. Don't worry about it. You needed a break. Now I need my *kaffi*."

She bit her lower lip. "Will you be able to work?"

"I have missed sleep in the past. It won't bother me. I've got to go do my chores." He rose and stretched out his arms.

Her breath seized and her heart started to hammer in her chest. How easy it would be to step into his embrace and have his arms enfold her.

Maisie quickly turned away and chided herself for her wayward thoughts. She had to get over this fascination with him before he noticed. "I'll go get changed."

She hurried up the stairs and pressed her hands to her flushed cheeks. There was nothing in Nathan's manner to suggest he would welcome or even understand her feelings if she made them known. How long could she keep them hidden?

The answer was simple. Forever.

Once she had her everyday work dress on, her hair up and her *kapp* pinned in place, she felt ready to face him again. She took a deep breath and went down to start breakfast. By the time he came in, she had oatmeal with brown sugar and raisins simmering on the stove, coffee ready in the pot and her emotions under control.

She sat at the table with her eyes down. If she didn't look at him it was easier to pretend nothing had changed. The oatmeal tasted like sawdust in her mouth.

"Do you need anything?" he asked. "Jimmy said he has to stop in town on his way home tonight."

She stirred a spoon of sugar into her coffee. She didn't even like it sweet. "Not that I can think of."

"You might check the machine later to see if anyone has answered my ad."

She nodded. "I will."

"Have I upset you?"

Maisie lifted her gaze to his face. "Of course not."

"Are you sure? You seem miles away."

"Too much sleep." She smiled, took a sip of her coffee and grimaced.

"Okay." He crossed to the cradles, knelt between them and laid his hands on each baby's head. "I'll miss you. May *Gott* bless and keep you both."

"Amen," Maisie said, watching his gentle goodbye.

He gazed at them and slowly shook his head.

"How is it that I can love them so much already?"

The sound of a truck pulling up and honking outside brought him to his feet. "I'd better go."

"Don't forget your lunch." She got up to hand him the small blue-and-white lunch pail. His hands brushed hers as he took it from her.

Nathan watched Maisie jerk her hand away and push it into her pocket. There was something different about her today. She seemed unhappy. Sad, even. He couldn't quite put his finger on it.

Jimmy sounded the horn again. Nathan had to leave, but he would get to the bottom of Maisie's unhappiness when he got home.

"Be safe today," she said. "I don't want to mend any more cuts in your pants."

"I'll do my best."

He went out and climbed into the front seat with his fellow logger. "Morning, Jimmy."

"Morning, Nate. How are the kids?"

Nathan grinned. "They are pretty amazing."

Jimmy turned the truck and drove down the lane. "That's what my girlfriend says, but I'm not convinced. Any success finding a gal to look after them?"

"Not yet."

"How much longer can your sister-in-law stay?"

"She says she's not going anywhere until I find someone."

"If she wants to stay, then why are you trying to hire someone else?"

"Because I don't want her staying longer than necessary."

"The two of you don't get along? I get it. I can't say I'm crazy about my girlfriend's family, either. I couldn't imagine her sister living with us if we get married. Yikes."

"*Ja*, that's the way of it." He didn't want to explain why having Annie's twin around was so painful. He was ashamed of the way his wife left him. He didn't want others to know how miserably he had failed as a husband. Thankfully, Jimmy didn't ask him anything else.

The trip up to Three Ponds logging camp was twenty miles one way. When they arrived, Nathan took off his black flat-topped hat and put on the hard hat that his boss required everyone to wear. Up here he didn't stick out as an Amish fellow. Many of the men had beards, as he did, though he didn't have a mustache. Even his suspenders weren't out of the ordinary. Many of the men wore them for comfort.

The day proved to be particularly grueling.

Nathan was felling trees as fast as he safely could, trying to do the work of two men. Davis hadn't been able to take on another feller yet. Nathan would be grateful when he did.

When quitting time rolled around, he wiped the sweat from his brow and knocked the sawdust off of his shirt and pants. He saw the rip in his sleeve where he had caught it on a broken branch. He was bringing more mending home for Maisie. He knew how to use a needle and thread, but her repairs were much neater than his.

Jimmy stopped in Fort Craig and left the truck to run several errands. Nathan noticed a bookstore across the street and got out. Inside, he easily found the children's section and purchased four books. Nothing could replace reading the Bible, but it would be nice to read something the children would come to enjoy as they grew older. He hoped Maisie would approve.

He was tired enough that he fell asleep in Jimmy's vehicle on the ride home. He didn't realize he was at his front door until Jimmy shook him by the arm. He sat up to see a green car drive away from his house. He didn't recognize it. He got out with the parcel he had purchased in town.

Maisie was standing on the front porch.

"Who was that?" he asked, nodding toward the car that had just driven away.

"Another applicant for your position. She wasn't suitable." Maisie turned and walked into the house.

"What makes you say that?" He followed her inside.

"Because she wasn't."

"You're gonna have to give a better reason than that." It occurred to him that she might have deliberately sent the woman away. She didn't want him to hire a nanny.

"She wasn't Amish."

He scowled. "I never said that was a requirement. Did she have experience?"

"She brought a résumé from her previous job, but I didn't care for her attitude."

"You're being deliberately vague. You could have asked her to wait another ten minutes and I could have spoken to her myself."

"It would've been a waste of your time and hers. I know the type of person who should be taking care of these babies and she wasn't it." Maisie walked to the sofa and sat down with her arms crossed tightly over her chest.

She was being deliberately infuriating. "You don't want me to hire anyone. No one will be the right kind of person in your eyes. You have taken advantage of my trust the same way your sister did."

Her eyes widened with shock. She surged to her feet. "If you feel that way you can call the woman and set up another interview. Her number is still on the answering machine. I'm going out. Make yourself something for supper. I'm tired of being your cook, bottle washer and housekeeper without getting a word of thanks. I don't know why I bother trying to please you. If those children didn't need me, I'd be gone today."

She stormed out of the house. He tossed his package on the sofa, collapsed into his chair and raked his hands through his hair. She was driving him to distraction. How much longer could he go on this way?

Fix his own supper? That wasn't a problem. He'd been cooking for himself for months. He got out of his chair and went to the kitchen to search the canned goods Maisie's friend had brought for something quick to eat. He could wash his own clothes and do his own mending, too, for that matter.

What did she mean when she said she was trying to please him? Why would she say that?

He found himself staring at an empty counter. Where had she put the jars and canned food? His storage space was limited and already full. Had she taken them out of the house to store them?

He looked around and noticed something under his open stairs. Walking over to investigate, he saw several neatly made shelves tucked underneath the stairwell. They were lined with all the canned produce the bishop's wife and Dinah Lapp had brought over.

It was a clever idea and a good use of his limited space. He fingered the rough-cut boards. It wouldn't take much for him to sand them smooth. A coat of paint and they would be as nice as store-bought. Who knew Annie's sister was handy with a hammer and a saw? Annie hadn't been.

Maisie must've learned the skills from her husband, or perhaps her father. He glanced toward the door. Maybe he had been too hard on her. She was helping him of her own free will and at no charge. He wouldn't be able to work at all if she hadn't been here. It annoyed him that he would have to apologize. Again.

Maisie wasn't paying attention to where she was going. She found a path in the woods leading away from the house and stayed on it. She wanted to get away from Nathan's accusing stare, from his constant comparisons to her sister. She wasn't Annie, but he would never see that.

He couldn't trust her because she was like her sister. She wasn't, but he wouldn't accept it. He thought she was capable of deceiving him.

Maybe she didn't want him to hire a caregiver for the babies, but that wasn't her reason for turning away a self-absorbed *Englisch* woman who couldn't stop checking her phone for five minutes.

He would discover the same thing for himself if he interviewed Ms. Harper. Would he admit Maisie was right about her? She doubted it. He would probably hire the woman just to spite her.

She didn't take notice of where she was until there was a small bridge in front of her that arched over a brook. It was made of small logs expertly joined together. It was Nathan's work. She knew that without being told.

She walked onto the bridge and stopped in the middle. She leaned on the railing to look into the water rushing by underneath. The babbling sound began to soothe her ragged nerves. Little by little she heard the sounds of the forest around her. The birds and the insects going about their lives on a warm summer evening. It was a special place. A place for lovers to stroll along and stop to kiss where she was standing.

It would be a wonderful spot to kiss someone she loved. She could almost imagine Nathan holding her close as the brook sang to them. How foolish was that thought?

"It's a pretty spot, isn't it?"

Maisie looked up to see Lilly Arnett standing on the path. "*Ja*, it is."

"Nathan built that bridge for me not long after he first arrived."

Maisie patted the solid railing. "I thought as much."

"How is he?" Lilly came onto the bridge and stood beside Maisie, looking into the water, as well.

"He's irritating, exasperating, closed-minded, stubborn and ungrateful."

Lilly threw back her head and laughed. It took Maisie a minute to see the humor in her litany of Nathan's shortcomings. She finally smiled.

Lilly leaned toward Maisie. "Enjoying your visit, are you?"

"With the babies, I am."

"Nathan doesn't get along with a lot of people. He prefers to be by himself. I understand that. I'm the same way. I wondered when I dropped you off at his place that night if he would welcome your help or send you packing."

"He drove me to the bus station the next morning," Maisie admitted with a wry smile.

"But you're still here."

"There wasn't a bus going south for three days."

Lilly chuckled. "We are remote in this part of the state. It's been longer than three days and yet here you stand."

"I'm staying. He can't make me leave." Maisie discovered a renewed sense of determination. "The babies are my sister's children. I promised to help take care of them. I didn't know that would be the last thing I said to her."

"I'm sorry for your loss. I never met her. I didn't know Nathan was married until I gave you a ride."

"They had been living apart." Maisie hoped that was enough of an explanation.

Lilly straightened. "Come down to my place. I'll fix us a cup of herbal tea and we can get better acquainted."

Maisie smiled at her. "I'd like that."

After an hour of tea, yummy butter cookies and quiet conversation, Lilly took Maisie on a tour of her extensive flower gardens, which included an abundance of wildflowers. Maisie happened to notice a glint of light through some overgrown ivy.

"What's that back there?"

Lilly looked to where she was pointing. "That used to be a caretaker's cottage when the place belonged to my grandparents. My in-laws used to stay there for the summers when my husband was alive. They are all gone now. I guess I should clean it up. It's too nice a place to let the ivy have it."

After another half hour of friendly chatter, Maisie bid her new friend goodbye and headed up the path. She had learned that Nathan had done odd jobs for Lilly in exchange for home-cooked meals when he'd first arrived. Clearing a path between the two homes had been his idea, so that Lilly didn't have to drive over to his place when she needed something. It was three miles by the winding road, but only three quarters of a mile though the woods.

Maisie stopped at the edge of the clearing when the cabin came into view. Light from the lamp over the kitchen table and from the one by the fireplace sent a warm glow spilling out the windows and the open doorway. It would be an inviting picture if she wasn't so uncertain of her welcome.

Maybe Nathan was right. It hadn't been intentional, but maybe she couldn't find someone suitable to care for the babies because she wanted so badly to care for them herself. From now on she would let him conduct the interviews and she would stay in the background.

She heard his voice before she reached the door. Pausing, she listened to him reading a story about a baby rabbit's adventures. When she stepped inside, she saw he had a babe in each arm while he balanced the book on his lap. He looked up at her.

"Don't stop," she said, coming in to sit down.

"Why don't you read? It's hard for me to turn the pages without jostling the babies."

"Okay." She took the book from him and looked at the colorful cover. "Where did you get this?"

"I stepped into the bookstore in town while Jimmy ran his errands tonight."

She sat back and began to read. "'Alejandro the cottontail spent many a wonderful hour in his rather small yard dreaming about the wonderful, spectacular thing he was destined to do one day. Of course he didn't know what that would be, but he had a spectacular imagination to match his spectacular name and he imagined all kinds of wonderful things.

"'What did a rather small rabbit imagine he could do? Well, one day he might rescue a beautiful princess and they would live in a towering castle.'"

Maisie read on through the imaginary adventures of the bunny until she came to the end of the story.

"'Late that night as Alejandro snuggled up to his mother's soft fur, she bent and kissed his forehead. Looking into her warm brown eyes, he whispered, "I love you, Mother."'

"'"Oh, Alejandro," his mother sighed. "That is the most wonderful, spectacular thing I have ever heard."'

"'Alejandro smiled happily as he drifted off to sleep. He had known all along that he would do something as wonderful and spectacular as his name. He just didn't know how simple it would be.'"

Maisie closed the book. "It's a very cute story."

"It's not an Amish story. But I liked the illustrations and I thought the children would, too, someday."

"I like the message, that telling someone you love them is the most wonderful, spectacular thing you can do."

"Can you take Charity?" he asked.

"Of course." Maisie laid the book aside and took the baby from his arm. He flexed his fingers and she smiled. "Pins and needles?"

"I should've put her down sooner, but I hated

to disturb her. She looks so peaceful and precious when she is sleeping."

Maisie laid Charity in her cradle while he settled Jacob in the other one. Nathan stood up straight and slipped his hands in his front pockets. "I was harsh earlier. I'm sorry."

"You might have been right. Maybe I didn't like either woman because I don't want to relinquish taking care of the twins."

"I fried a can of pressed pork for supper. Would you like some?"

"I'm not hungry. I met Lilly Arnett on my walk. She fed me tea and butter cookies."

"She always has some on hand for visitors, although she claims she likes living alone. I wanted to tell you that I like your idea for extra storage under the stairs."

She glanced that way. "It's not meant to be permanent. I needed a place to store the canned goods so I could have my kitchen counter back. I mean, your kitchen counter," she added hastily. He stood so close that she could reach out and touch him if she dared. She curled her fingers into her palms.

"You're handy with a saw and hammer. Was it your father who taught you?"

"My husband. I was curious about the things he built. He didn't mind teaching me." In his way, John had been kind to her, but not loving.

"You must've paid attention. It's sturdy." Nathan picked up the book. "I bought several like this. Would you want to see them?"

"Certainly." Maisie relaxed as he stepped away from her and picked up the books on the mantel. He handed them to her. They were all stories about baby animals with problems to solve.

Nathan's and her problems weren't solved, but at least they weren't arguing. It was a small step in the right direction.

She gave the books back to him. "You'll have to build a bookshelf for them when they are old enough to read."

He looked around the room. "Where would I put it?"

"In their bedroom, I guess, or there in the corner beside the fireplace."

"I like the idea of having it out here where I can watch them. A family should spend time together."

Maisie smiled at his enthusiasm. "I doubt that will be a problem as you only have one room in your house."

"For now, but I'll add on as they grow. I've thought about lifting the roof and adding a second story with several bedrooms."

He was looking to the future. Maisie was

glad he could. He was healing. A bigger house might mean a bigger family. A wife and other children.

And no need for an aunt.

Chapter Ten

The rest of the week passed in a blur for Nathan. His workdays were long and tiring without the additional helper Davis had promised. He had breakfast with Maisie, kissed his children goodbye and didn't return home until almost dark.

Maisie took over his evening chores, feeding the animals, cleaning stalls and making sure the livestock and poultry were secured at night. She didn't ask. She just started doing it. Because of her, he had a free hour in the evenings to spend reading to the babies or simply holding them before heading to bed.

On Saturday, he worked ten hours for some much-needed overtime pay, but he told himself it was the last time. He didn't want to spend that much time away from his children again if it could be helped.

No one else responded to his ads for child-care. He had to face the fact that he still needed Maisie's help.

Sunday brought the event he dreaded most since Annie's funeral. His first prayer meeting with all the members of his new Amish community. He might have stayed home if he had been on his own, but Maisie insisted that he take her.

She was up when he entered the cabin and had breakfast waiting for him. Afterward, she gathered together the pies and cookies she had baked the night before and loaded them into a cardboard box for him to put in the buggy. There would be a meal after the three- or four-hour-long service and every family would bring something to contribute.

After loading the food, he came back in to help her with the babies.

She didn't glance his way. "Jacob is ready to go. I'm going to have to change Charity's gown. She spit up on this one."

"Are you worried about meeting more members of the community?" he asked.

"*Nee*, why should I be?"

Because I am. "No reason."

"Go on," she said. "I'll be there in a minute." She wore a white apron over a dark green dress. It was a color Annie had often worn.

She once said it made her eyes look greener. He thought it was a vain reason. Was that why Maisie chose the same shade?

Why wouldn't she share her sister's vanity? They were twins.

He carried Jacob in his basket out to the buggy and settled him on the front seat. The buggy itself had been washed and swept out. Sassy had been groomed until her coat was as shiny black as a raven's wing. Her harness had been oiled and the brass fittings polished. His rig hadn't looked this good since he'd bought it. He might not be a man of means, but he wasn't ashamed of what he had.

He got in, picked up the lines and waited. He was about to call to Maisie when she came rushing out the door. "I hope I haven't made us late."

"We have plenty of time. It isn't far to the Fisher place."

"What do you know about them?" Maisie asked as she settled herself and Charity.

Nathan spoke to Sassy to get her moving. "Walk on. The father is a wheelwright. He has four sons. One of them is a harness maker. The others work with him."

"Are they married?" she asked.

He glanced her way. Was she hoping to find a husband in New Covenant? She had been a widow for more than two years. There was no reason why she couldn't remarry. "The oldest is. Gabriel, he's the harness maker. He goes by Gabe. He's married to Esther. One of the other sons is married, too, but I don't know which one."

"Have you decided on the story we should tell people about Annie's death? The truth is always best, of course. Still, I thought we should compare what we will say."

"I reckon so." She was right but he hated thinking about it. The bishop knew the whole story. Nathan had explained his situation in confidence when he asked Bishop Schultz to perform Annie's private burial service. Why did he have to say anything to the others? Why couldn't it be his business and no one else's?

Maisie folded her hands in her lap. "You and Annie were married in Seymour, Missouri, where she and I grew up. You came to Maine to start a new life. Annie was on her way to join you when she went into labor, delivered the babies and died of complications before she reached you. That is all true."

"What if someone asks why it took her so long to join me? They know I've been here for months."

"Then you will have to answer as you see

fit. Not every marriage is a happy one. People know that."

"Was yours?"

Her startled gaze shot to his then she looked away. "For the most part. It's not possible to be happy all the time."

"Did you ever think about leaving him?"

"*Nee*, the idea never crossed my mind. I was married to John for better or for worse, no matter what problems we encountered."

"Why do you think Annie left me?"

Maisie's gaze returned to him. "Didn't her notes say that she had tried to live Amish, but she couldn't do it anymore?"

"That never made sense. I know she liked working for that *Englisch* family, but she never complained about giving up electricity or television or riding in fast cars after she stopped working for them. Did she ever mention that to you?"

Maisie shook her head. "I didn't see much of her after you were married. I know she missed the children that she had been taking care of. She was very close to the family."

"She didn't tell them she was leaving."

"As far as I know she didn't tell anyone. She didn't even tell me. I thought we shared everything."

She finally looked at him. "That is all in the

past and can't be changed. We should leave it there."

If only that was possible. He would wonder until his dying day what had gone wrong.

The traffic was light on the highway and they saw no other buggies. There weren't any Amish families beyond his place. Sassy kept up a steady trot without urging. They arrived at the Fisher farm only thirty minutes after leaving home. They weren't the first. A dozen buggies were already parked along the lane. The horses, still wearing their harnesses, were busy munching hay, swishing their tails or dozing where they were tied to a white wooden corral fence.

The bishop's buggy was parked beside the barn, along with the gray enclosed wagon that carried the benches they would use. The backless wooden benches were transported to the family that was hosting the prayer meeting to provide enough seating.

Nathan had heard of a new Amish settlement a hundred miles south of Fort Craig that used a permanent building for their church meetings, but the New Covenant Amish still met for worship in members' homes every other Sunday, the way the Amish had done since the days of their persecution before coming to America in the 1700s.

He pulled up outside the front-yard gate. Three women came out to meet Maisie. He recognized the two women he'd met at his house. He didn't know the other woman. She was young with red hair, a babe in her arms and a toddler holding on to her skirt. Dinah Lapp introduced her as her daughter, Gemma Crump. Maisie was soon surrounded by more women and children all wanting to see the twins.

"I'll take your horse and buggy."

Nathan turned to see a boy of about fifteen at his window. The lad grinned. "I'm Harvey Gingrich. My oldest brother, Willis, is a blacksmith in New Covenant. I know who you are. What's your mare's name?"

Nathan wondered what the boy knew about him. "Sassy. I have a grain bag for her in the back. You can put it on her now. *Danki*."

Harvey moved to take Sassy by the bridle. He patted her neck. "I'll take *goot* care of her."

"*Vellkumm*, Nathan Weaver." The oldest son of the Fisher family came toward him. His eyes were full of sympathy, but he didn't mention Nathan's loss.

Nathan nodded to him. "Morning, Gabe."

"Give us a hand unloading the benches, will you?"

"Sure." Nathan would have offered without

being asked, but he appreciated Gabe's attempt to include him. A man pulling a bench out turned around to greet Gabe. He was clearly Gabe's sibling.

Gabe tipped his head toward him. "My brother Seth."

"You're twins?" Nathan asked.

"Triplets, although our brother Asher doesn't look like us. He has dark hair like our little brother, Moses. We heard you have twins. Congratulations," Gabe said.

Seth grinned. "The best part of being a twin was fooling folks as to which of us was which when we were kids."

"I have a boy and a girl. I shouldn't have trouble telling them apart," Nathan said with a small grin.

Gabe chuckled and clapped Nathan on the shoulder. "Let's hope not. Grab that end of the bench and I'll get the other."

"Where are we going?" Nathan asked, as barns, sheds and outbuildings were often used for large worship gatherings.

"We're a small congregation yet, so we all fit in the house," Gabe said.

Nathan nodded and lifted out the next bench. For the next twenty minutes he met more of the men from the New Covenant Amish community. Only one, a man named Tully Lange, gripped Nathan's hand and offered his condolences. An older man with Tully touched his shoulder and shook his head. Tully seemed surprised but walked away.

The older man leaned heavily on a cane. "I'm Gideon Beachy. My son-in-law isn't familiar with all our ways. He's newly come to the Amish. I will explain to him that we seldom mention the dead once a funeral is over. To do so may be seen as questioning *Gott*'s will."

Nathan knew he was still questioning. "Tell Tully I appreciate his sympathy."

"I shall. *Vellkumm* to New Covenant. I think you'll find we are all *goot* neighbors and friends. I see the bishop and the ministers going in. Must be time for the service to start."

Nathan followed Gideon inside. The older man took a seat in one of the family's overstuffed chairs that had been set up beside a row of benches.

The seating was separated into two columns with an aisle between. Men and women sat separately. Nathan took his place among the married men sitting on the first few benches at the front, and picked up the black hymnal that had been set out for him. Behind him sat a row of beardless young unmarried men. In the last row on the men's side, the youngest boys were seated closest to the door, ready to make a quick exit when the service was over.

On the other side of the aisle were the women. He caught sight of Maisie in between two young mothers with children beside them. She seemed at ease. He didn't doubt that she had answered more questions about their situation than he had. It seemed to him that women were more curious about others than men were.

The *volsinger*, or song leader, a man near the front of the room, announced the hymn. The rustling of hymnals being opened and pages being turned filled the quiet space. When the sound faded, the man began the first hymn in a loud clear voice, and everyone joined in.

There was no musical accompaniment to an Amish prayer service. There were only voices of the faithful solemnly praising God in slow, mournful tones. The lyrics of the song were written in the hymnal Nathan held, but there were no musical notes to follow. The hymns had been handed down through countless generations, always sung from memory.

Nathan joined in the song and found a surprising peace in recalling the words he had sung since he was old enough to talk. He glanced at Maisie. She had her eyes downcast as she sang. He could just pick out her voice. Slightly off-key, but filled with enthusiasm.

How many times had he cast his eyes toward Annie during the service when he first saw her? She had been so pretty, she'd taken his breath away. If Maisie had been there he didn't remember seeing her, but she would have been sitting with the married women, like she was today.

When the last words of the song died away, the bishop and two other men entered the front of the room. They would share the preaching, taking turns throughout the next three or four hours.

Nathan glanced at Maisie again, wondering how she would fare with both babies to look after for all that time. He didn't need to worry. Less than an hour into the service another babe in the room started fussing. The young mother sent her toddler across the aisle to her father, a big burly man with black hair sitting in front of Nathan. Maisie and the other mother took their infants from the room. He heard them going upstairs.

Maisie followed Gemma to a bedroom at the end of the hall on the second story. The window was open to the morning breeze, which carried in the scent of roses. Crossing to the window, Maisie looked down and saw a trellis below heavily laden with the red, fragrant blooms. "I wondered how flowers would do this far north, but I see Mrs. Fisher has a lovely garden."

"The winters are harsh. Our summers are short, but the summer days are long this far north. That gives flowers and vegetables plenty of sunlight. It isn't a forgiving land, but it can be bountiful."

Maisie turned away from the window. "How old is your son?"

"Three months."

Maisie grinned. "He's big for his age."

"I know. He takes after his father. My daughter was premature, so I'm not used to lugging such a big fellow around. How old are the twins?"

"Two weeks." Maisie sat down on one of the twin beds in the room and lifted Jacob out of his basket, then began to change his diaper. He kicked happily.

"They grow up too fast," Gemma said with a sad smile. "It must be difficult for you. Coming so far and not finding a warm welcome from their father. Dinah told me about your situation."

"I will treasure every moment I have with them. When Nathan hires a nanny, I will look for a job of my own. I intend to stay in New Covenant. They are my sister's children, and

I can't leave them. I know she wouldn't want me to."

"There is plenty of work during the potato harvest, but I'm afraid over the winter it may be harder to find a job. The area is very rural. The Amish here don't have little shops and home businesses the way they do in other communities where tourism brings in lots of people. The reason New Covenant was founded was to avoid the temptations that come with tourism and allow Amish families to tend the land the way it used to be."

"Then your husband must be a farmer."

"Jesse and I raise potatoes for our main cash crop, but also hay and oats for our animals. For a while he worked for Bishop Schultz building garden sheds, but since we were able to acquire more land Jesse now farms full-time. It's nice to have him close by to help when I need him. Is Nathan going to stop working for Arthur Davis?"

"Not anytime soon. He has hospital bills to pay."

"I'm sure the church will help with his bills. They helped me and my husband pay for Grace's medical care."

"Nathan feels that because he isn't a member of this congregation he shouldn't ask for their assistance."

Gemma scowled at Maisie. "That's ridiculous. We help any Amish family in need. Our church has sent donations to those affected by tragedies in many states."

"Someone else will have to persuade him of that because he won't listen to me."

Gemma arched one eyebrow. "Stubborn, is he?"

Maisie smiled. "A little."

Gemma chuckled. "I'll have my husband speak to him and perhaps the bishop can. There's no shame in needing help. That goes for you, too. Taking care of little ones can be exhausting. Especially twins. Any one of us would be happy to take over and give you a few hours rest since Nathan won't be at home."

"*Danki.* I do miss my sleep."

"I know it isn't always possible, but I think it's best when a father doesn't have to leave the farm for work. Our families are second only to God in importance."

Maisie smiled at the baby she held. "I couldn't agree more."

"I hate to see you being separated from them. Are you sure Nathan won't relent and allow you to be their *kinder heeda*?"

"I'm sure he won't. Besides, it may be for the best."

Gemma's eyes narrowed. "Why would you say that?"

"It just would." Tears pricked the backs of Maisie's eyes. She quickly blinked them back. Her feelings for Nathan weren't something she could talk about. It didn't seem right to harbor such affection for her sister's husband.

"I think my boy is finished. May I feed your little girl?" Gemma asked.

Maisie managed a smile. "Please do. Her bottle is in the bag with her."

After the babies were fed, the women returned to the prayer meeting. Maisie kept her eyes down, resisting the urge to see if Nathan was looking her way. When simply talking about him made her eyes tear up she couldn't risk meeting his gaze. She didn't want him to suspect how much she had come to care for him.

When the service ended, Bishop Schultz faced everyone. "I have one announcement to make. We have a new family joining our community. Peter Yoder, his wife and their twelve children. Peter has purchased the home south of Gideon Beachy's dairy, but it isn't big enough for his family, so we are having a work frolic to build an addition onto his house this coming Saturday. Leroy Lapp has a list of needed supplies so check with him."

As everyone filed out, Maisie stayed in the house to help ready the meal along with several other women. She caught sight of Nathan waiting for her by the door. When he started toward her, she fought down the urge to run in the opposite direction.

"Aren't you ready to go?" he asked.

"I must help serve the meal." Around her, the men were rearranging the benches and stacking them into tables where people could eat.

Nathan nodded toward the door. "Others can do that."

"I don't want people to think I am a slacker. I will do my part. We can leave once the meal is over. If you are afraid to stay longer I'm sure someone can give the children and myself a ride home later."

"I'm not afraid to stay. I just don't like standing around talking. It's pointless."

She could tell from his tone that he wasn't happy. Neither was she. He was being ridiculous, and her patience was growing thin. She wanted him to leave her alone. "Then sit in a corner and pout until I'm done."

His frown deepened, then he turned on his

heel and left. She wanted to call him back and apologize but maybe it was better if they stayed at odds with each other.

So much for her plan to be kinder to him.

Bishop Schultz was coming in the door as Nathan was going out. "Nathan, I'm delighted to see you. I'm glad you could join us."

He didn't say it was about time, but Nathan heard the words the bishop left unspoken. "Maisie was keen to come." He should have let her come alone.

"My wife had only *goot* things to say about meeting her."

Nathan didn't want to talk about Maisie. The woman was exasperating. "Have you found anyone to take care of my children?"

"I confess I have not. Why don't you want your sister-in-law to stay?"

Nathan glanced over his shoulder. "We don't get along."

"I'm sorry to hear that. Division in a family is never a good thing. Most often it is the children who suffer because of it."

The bishop laid his hand on Nathan's shoulder. "I know you don't want that. Do what you can to mend your differences before it affects the children."

"I don't think we can."

Bishop Shultz bent forward to look into Nathan's eyes. "Are you sure it isn't bitterness toward your late wife that makes you say that? Her actions wounded you deeply and you will never know the reason for her choices. Forgiveness must come first, even before understanding. That is the cornerstone of our faith. You will not know peace until that happens."

"I'm afraid that's easier said than done."

"Only because you aren't yet willing to make that commitment. When you are ready, forgiveness will come easily. I must ask you one more question. It, too, may not have an easy answer."

"What?"

"Are you being fair to Maisie? Think on it. I hope to see you at the frolic."

Chapter Eleven

Nathan wanted to ignore the bishop's words, but the harder he tried to forget them, the more they stuck in his mind. Was he being fair to Maisie?

Maybe he wasn't, but he didn't want to be constantly reminded of Annie, either. He couldn't see a way to reconcile his dilemma. He couldn't escape thinking about her even when she was out of his sight.

"Nathan, have you got a minute?" Gabe asked, beckoning to him from across the driveway.

"Sure." Nathan walked toward him.

Gabe gestured toward the building that was attached to the side of the barn. "You've been in my workshop. You bought your harness from me."

"I did and I'm pleased with it."

"Glad to hear that. I've been thinking about expanding the place. I'm considering a log addition. I know you built your home from logs. I was wondering what the drawbacks would be."

Nathan pushed his relationship with Maisie to the back of his mind. He slipped his hands into his front pockets and rocked back on his heels. "You won't find many drawbacks to log construction. Well-fitted logs provide plenty of insulation to keep it cool in the summer and warm in the winter. You can hang hooks for your merchandise anywhere on the walls. If you have your own trees, as I did, the only lumber you have to purchase is for the roof, windows and doors. In addition, a peeled and polished log interior is attractive without needing any paneling or paint. A coat of varnish will make the natural color last a long time."

At this point Gabe's dad, Zeke, had joined them. "We would need someone to point out which trees we should harvest."

"I could do that for you," Nathan said. "I'd advise against using them this season. It's best to let them dry out over the winter. Are you in a hurry to expand?"

Zeke chuckled. "My sons are always in a hurry. Why don't you take a look around our forest and see if we have trees that are worth harvesting before we take the idea any further."

"I've started back to work for Arthur Davis so it will have to be next weekend before I can get out here."

Zeke looked at Gabe and then nodded. "That's agreeable."

"If you have the right kind of timber, will you cut it yourself or will you need a logger?" Nathan asked, hoping for a little extra income.

Gabe lifted his hat and combed back his blond hair with his fingers. He settled his hat on again and looked at Nathan. "We can't conduct business on Sunday. We'll discuss that when you come to look over our trees. How about a game of horseshoes? Cowboy can join us. He loves the game."

Nathan cocked his head to the side. "Cowboy?"

"That's what we call Tully. He was an Oklahoma cowboy before he found us. Ask him to show you some of his rope tricks."

"Is he any good?" Nathan asked.

Gabe laughed. "He was an *Englischer* who roped himself an Amish wife. That takes real skill."

"If he has joined our faith, I'd say it was the wife who possessed considerable talent in bringing him around."

"Nee." Zeke shook his head. "Tully says *Gott* used Becca to give his life purpose. The

Lord makes use of us all in ways we may never know."

Maisie came out of the house and walked toward Nathan. He focused on the ground. She stopped a few feet away. "I'm ready to go if you are."

He cleared his throat. "Spend some time with your new friends. I can wait."

"Are you sure?" she asked hopefully.

"*Ja*. We will go when everyone is done eating."

"*Danki*. I'm sorry about earlier."

"Forget it."

She gave him a tight smile before she turned and walked back to the house.

Nathan looked up to find Gabe staring at him. His father was heading toward the barn. Gabe arched one eyebrow. "Trouble between you and Maisie?"

"What makes you think that?"

Gabe shrugged. "My wife, Esther, is deaf, and she's very good at reading body language. I've picked up a thing or two from her."

Nathan sighed. "Maisie is my wife's identical twin."

"So?" Gabe asked.

Nathan wanted someone to understand what he was going through. Gabe was a twin. Perhaps he could see Nathan's point. "It's like looking at the woman I lost every time I see her."

"I take it you didn't know Maisie well before this?"

"I saw her briefly at the wedding and a few times at different gatherings." He'd only had eyes for Annie back then.

"As a triplet I can say my brothers and I are confused by people who don't know us well. We may look alike at first glance, but we're totally different people. Your grief is new, Nathan. It colors your thinking. That's only natural. As you get to know Maisie better you'll see that she isn't so much like her sister. Come on." Gabe tipped his head toward the barn. "The horseshoe pit is this way."

Nathan thoroughly enjoyed himself for the next hour as he and Gabe played against Zeke and Tully. He didn't have their skill level. He hadn't played in a while, but everyone looked like amateurs when the bishop played against the big black-haired fellow Nathan learned was Jesse Crump. Both men were highly skilled, but the bishop inched out a win at the end of three games. The older men congratulated the bishop while Gabe, Nathan, Tully and the other Fisher brothers commiserated with Jesse.

"Admit it," Moses said. "You let him win."

A wry grin appeared on Jesse's face. "You

will never hear those words from my lips. It's my opinion that the Lord is on the bishop's side." He slapped Nathan on the back. "I hear you're a lumberjack. Kind of small for that line of work, aren't you?"

Nathan stood several inches taller than the Fisher brothers, but he didn't come close to Jesse's height. "With a sharp chain saw in hand the tree doesn't care how big the man is. It falls just the same."

Gabe laughed. "Jesse doesn't use a chain saw. He just bites the trees off and uses the splinters for toothpicks."

Jesse took the teasing good-naturedly. "Sometimes it takes two bites. Walnut is a lot harder than pine."

Nathan realized he had missed the camaraderie of other Amish men since leaving Missouri. He had friends among his *Englisch* coworkers in the lumber company, but there was something special about the dry wit of Amish men that another Amish fellow could appreciate.

"I had best round up my family and head for home," Tully said. "The cows haven't learned how to milk themselves." He walked over and spoke to his father-in-law and then to Harvey. The boy nodded and jogged toward the horses.

He untied one and led it to one of the parked buggies.

Nathan looked toward the house. Maisie was probably becoming impatient. He walked into the kitchen and heard voices coming from the living room. He looked in and saw her sitting cross-legged on the floor. She was holding Charity against her shoulder while Jacob lay snuggled in the nest of her lap. Two young girls, who looked to be eight or nine, were lying on the floor with their chins propped on their hands beside Maisie, admiring Jacob. Maisie was chuckling at the antics of the toddler playing peekaboo with a teenage girl in the center of the room.

Maisie looked up and caught sight of him. Her bright smile vanished. Because of him. He suddenly wished he knew how to restore it. What did the others think of their relationship?

"I'm ready if you are," he said, avoiding her eyes.

"I am. Annabeth and Maddie, would you fetch the baskets for the babies?"

The girls beside her popped to their feet and raced up the stairs. Maisie held Charity out for Nathan to take, then transferred Jacob to her arms and rose.

The two girls came downstairs and set the baskets at Maisie's feet. She settled Jacob in one then held out her arms for Charity. Nathan handed over his daughter. Maisie swaddled her and tucked her in. "There we go, *liebling*. Snug as a bug," she said softly.

Maisie was so at ease handling them. She seemed at home with the other women in the room, too. He felt oddly out of place and wondered if they had been talking about him.

He picked up Jacob's basket. "We'll be in the buggy."

"I won't be a moment. Goodbye, everyone."

"Don't forget to let us know if you need anything," Gemma said. "We'll be out to check on you soon."

Nathan paused in the doorway when he heard that. Check on her? Why?

Maisie nodded. "I appreciate that. I'll see you then."

"Bethany will bring some of her cinnamon biscuits because I love them," Gemma said.

"You should learn to make them yourself," another woman said. Nathan recognized her as Bethany Shetler. They'd met on the day he was taking Maisie to the bus station.

Gemma sighed heavily. "I've tried. Yours are better."

"I'll fix cinnamon coffee to go with them," Maisie said.

"*Ach*, that sounds *goot*. How is it made?" the bishop's wife asked.

Maisie glanced at Nathan and then back to the women. "I'll show you when you come. Goodbye."

Outside, he found Harvey had brought Sassy and his buggy to the front door. Nathan helped Maisie in and then handed her Jacob. He went around to the driver's side and got in. "Why are they coming out to check on you?"

"Because that's what they do for new mothers. I know I'm not the children's mother but taking care of them and the house can be exhausting. The women will clean and bring ready-made meals so I don't have to cook as much." She settled Jacob's basket next to Charity on the seat so that both babies were between them.

"That's *goot*. I won't be so concerned about you while I'm at work."

Her gaze snapped to his. "You don't need to worry. I'll take every care with them."

"Oh, I know that." In fact, he was sure of it. He picked up the lines and clicked his tongue to get Sassy moving.

Maisie watched the slowly changing countryside as Sassy trotted toward Nathan's home. Fields of potato plants were sandwiched between areas of dense forest, giving the land a patchwork appearance in varying shades of green. There were a few wheat fields and cornfields, too, but for the most part the farmable land grew potatoes. It was the staple crop for the area.

She looked at the babies, who were both sleeping peacefully, and smiled. The worship service and the companionship of new friends had succeeded in lifting her spirits. She glanced at Nathan, determined to keep things casual between them. "I thought all three of the preachers did a *goot* job, didn't you?"

"*Ja.*"

He didn't elaborate. "Did I miss anything important while I was upstairs with the *kinder*?"

"*Nee.*"

"Was meeting people as hard as you feared?"

"It wasn't."

Two words that time. He was getting quite talkative. "No one asked about my sister. I think Constance and Dinah must have shared what I told them with everyone. Did anyone ask you about Annie?"

"I spoke to the bishop. He knows the whole story. Only Tully Lange offered his condolences and asked about her. His father-in-law was quick to explain that Tully was newly come to our faith and didn't know it was improper to speak of the dead."

"His wife Becca told me Tully was *Englisch*. I've never known one of them to join our faith, have you?"

"I have not."

Maisie stared at her folded hands. "I guess I shouldn't mention Annie anymore. *Gott* allowed her death. I accept that, but I'm not ready to let her go. We were so close once."

"If you need to talk about her I will understand," he said, surprising Maisie.

"Danki."

Not knowing what else to say, she went back to watching the landscape. In the distance, she saw a black shape loping up the side of a hill.

She sat up straight. "Is that a bear?"

Nathan looked her way. "Where?"

"Near the top of that rise?" She pointed to where she was looking.

"I see it. That's a black bear, all right."

Nathan's home was less than a mile away. "Are they dangerous?"

"They avoid people so make noise if you are walking in the woods."

"What do you mean make noise? What kind of noise?"

"Talking, singing. Anything to let the animal know where you are."

"I'll remember that. I should climb a tree if I see one, right?" She shivered at the idea. What if she was out with the children?

"They are excellent climbers so that won't deter them."

Walking in the woods was definitely out of the question now. "Have you seen them near your home?"

"Occasionally. Buddy will warn them away if they come around."

"He's not a very big dog."

"His bark is loud enough. I reckon mine has been, too. For that I'm sorry."

Was he apologizing for the times he had snapped at her? "At least you don't bite."

"I'll do better in the future."

"As will I."

A smile pulled up one corner of his mouth. "Haven't we had this conversation already?"

"You less irritated and me less annoying? I believe we have."

"Perhaps we'll get it right if we keep trying."

"I'll be less irritated from now on. You can be less annoying."

"It's a deal."

Jacob began crying. Maisie tried to soothe him but he wasn't having it. She hadn't packed more formula because she thought Nathan would have returned home by now. Nathan turned into his lane and Sassy picked up the pace. He stopped her in front of the cabin.

Maisie picked up Jacob and his head bobbed angrily against her shoulder as he tried to find something to suck on. His grasping hand found the ribbon on her *kapp* and he pulled it toward his mouth.

Maisie winced and tipped her head. "Ow! Stop, honey, that's pinned to my hair." She tried to open his fist, but he hung on tight, pulled harder and yelled at the top of his lungs.

"Let me help." Nathan opened her door and leaned in. He took hold of the baby's hand. His own fingers brushed against Maisie's neck. "Let go, *sohn*," he coaxed.

Maisie felt the heat rush to her face at Nathan's nearness. "It's fine. I can manage."

"I've got it." He gave a tug that pulled her *kapp* crookedly over her eye, but the babe let loose.

Nathan tried to smooth her head covering back in place. Suddenly he paused with one hand still touching her face. Maisie looked into his eyes and saw confusion. Her heart began to beat faster. What did he see? What was he thinking? Was he remembering the times he had touched Annie's face with tenderness? She looked away, but the feelings she held in her heart didn't subside. If anything, they grew stronger. She didn't want to be the cause of his pain or a reminder of sweet things that passed between a husband and wife.

She wanted Nathan to see *her*. She could tell he didn't.

A knot formed in Nathan's chest. Maisie's hair was thick and soft. The sun-dried smell of her linen *kapp* mixed with the scents of lavender and clean babies. He realized he was looming over her when she pulled away. He slowly withdrew his hand and took a step back. "He's got a good grip for such a small fellow. He'll be able to hold an axe, for sure."

She cradled the crying boy in her arms and slipped out of the buggy without speaking. Her shoulder brushed against Nathan's chest, causing the knot in him to tighten. He took another step back and watched her rush into the house. Once she was out of sight, he was able to take a breath.

His reaction to Maisie's nearness amazed him. It should have been because she resembled his wife, but he hadn't been thinking about Annie in that moment.

He couldn't be attracted to Maisie. The idea was ridiculous. Besides being his sister-in-law, she didn't even like him.

He shook his head to clear it. His reaction

had to be because she looked like Annie. The affection he'd had for his wife had withered during the months following her vanishing act, but he had loved her once. The moment with Maisie must have sparked the memory of those tender feelings. He would have to take care that it didn't happen again.

Charity began to squirm in her carrier. Nathan realized he'd forgotten about her. He lifted her out of the basket and cuddled her against his chest. "Sorry, *liebling*. Your *daed* isn't thinking straight today."

She curled into a ball against him. So tiny and precious. His heart expanded with love for her. "May *Gott* grant me the strength to protect you always."

Would her life be difficult without a mother? Nathan could supply many of her needs, but what about the things a little girl learned at her mother's knee? How to cook and sew and make a home, even how to care for younger brothers and sisters. All these things, and so many others, he wouldn't be able to teach her. Perhaps her nanny, when he hired one, would show her all those things.

He glanced toward the house. Maisie could teach her what she needed to know and would love her, too. Every child needed to be loved.

The bishop's words came back to him again.

He was being unfair to Maisie, but was he being unfair to his children, too? Didn't they deserve to be loved by her?

He shook his head and kissed the top of his daughter's bonnet. "Your *kinder heeda* will love you and your brother. How could she not?"

He walked into the house determined to avoid a repeat of his closeness with Maisie. Dredging up old memories of Annie was exactly why he didn't want Maisie around.

The afternoon passed pleasantly enough. He thought Maisie took pains to stay out of his way. She cooked a light supper of boiled beef and cabbage from his garden. He liked the way she seasoned it. He couldn't recall Annie ever making the dish.

After supper, he got down the Bible and sat in the rocking chair between the babies to read to them. Maisie sat at the kitchen table mending his socks. He didn't have a pair without at least one hole in them. He was grateful she had noticed.

After half an hour, he closed the book. Maisie looked up from her mending. "Shall I fix you a lunch for tomorrow?"

"I can eat at the canteen on site. You don't need to go to any trouble."

"Is the food *goot*?"

"It's food."

"I see. So, *ja*, I will fix you a lunch." Her tone said the subject was closed. She put her mending aside. "I believe I will turn in now."

"I think I'll stay up a while. I like to watch them sleep. You don't have to stay up with me," he added quickly.

She smiled softly. "Remain as long as you like."

"*Danki*, Maisie. For all you have done for my babies," he said, wanting her to know he meant it.

She smiled at him. "It's what Annie would have wanted me to do." She crossed the room and climbed the stairs to the loft.

The bishop's question came back to Nathan. *Are you being fair to Maisie?*

He wasn't. He wasn't being fair to his children, either.

He should let Maisie be their nanny, but how was he going to make that work?

Chapter Twelve

Maisie was relieved when the weekend was over and Nathan started back to work again. It meant she only had to see him for brief times during the day. She fixed his breakfast and his lunch with a cheerful smile on her face. It wasn't until he went out the door that she fell to pieces. She tried to put him out of her mind, but it was like making the sun go down in the east. Impossible.

When she was with him, she noticed everything about him, from the way he smiled at his babies to the way he didn't smile at her. It was hopeless. He was growing dearer to her every single day.

The evenings were the worst, when he read to the babies or worked on some project at the kitchen table. Sometimes she caught him watching her and her heart would begin to race, but he always looked away. He never said that he cared for her, too. She took to going up to bed early just so she wouldn't have to face him and hide her feelings.

She longed for and yet dreaded the coming weekend, when he would be home for two whole days.

Friday evening she sat in the rocker after supper and picked up Charity. The babe wasn't hungry so Maisie just rocked her and hummed a children's song she had learned when she was in school.

"I remember that one," Nathan said. He was sitting in his chair with an open book in his lap.

"I think all schoolchildren must learn it." She traced Charity's dainty eyebrow with the tip of her finger.

"Davis finally hired another feller. The man is every bit as good as Ricky was."

"I'm glad to hear that."

He cleared his throat nervously. "I've been reconsidering your situation here."

She stopped rocking. "What does that mean?"

"It means I've decided that you should be their *kinder heeda*. I'm not going to look for anyone else."

She could barely believe her ears. "Do you mean it?"

"I have to think about what's best for them. It's clear you love them. You're a sensible woman. I think you're the best person for the job."

Tears sprang to Maisie's eyes. "Oh, Nathan, how can I thank you?"

"You've been caring for them and doing it well in spite of my objections. You might as well be paid for the position."

Her heart was so full of joy that she didn't know what to say. She bent and kissed Charity on the cheek. "Do you hear that? I'm going to take care of you for as long as you and your brother need me."

"We should discuss living arrangements." Nathan rubbed his hand nervously on the arm of his chair.

"Okay."

"You can't continue staying here. It was understandable when you first arrived, but now you will need your own place."

He didn't want her here. He had made that abundantly clear from the start. It shouldn't hurt to hear him say it again, but it did. "How will you manage to take care of them through the night and still work if I'm not here?"

"I've been thinking about that. If you agree,

the babies can spend the nights with you through the week and then with me over the weekend. Say Friday, Saturday and Sunday nights."

"That sounds reasonable. I'll have to start looking for a place to rent. Nathan, I can't tell you how happy this makes me."

"Then all we have to do is agree on your salary."

"I can't take money for watching my niece and nephew."

"You can't live on air. I don't know how you are set financially, but I suspect you aren't wealthy."

That made her laugh. "Hardly."

"Then you must treat this as a paying position. Will you be going to the frolic tomorrow?"

"Of course. And you?"

"It's time I started helping my fellow man again. I've been holed up for long enough."

"I'm glad to hear you say that." It was what she wanted for him. For him to move forward with his life and leave the bitterness and unhappiness behind.

"I reckon I'll see you early in the morning, then." He rose and left the cabin, taking Buddy with him.

Maisie got to her feet and twirled around

once, still holding Charity in her arms. "Do you hear that? I'm going to be taking care of you forever. Or until you start school, whichever comes first. You know what this means? It means your father is accepting me as part of his family." It wasn't what her heart desired, but it was close enough.

Nathan nailed another sheet of siding in place on the new addition for Peter Yoder's home. All around him, men were working in concert to complete the project by the end of the day. Gabe came down from his place on the roof. "We're almost done."

"It was a good day's work," Nathan said. He paused to look for Maisie and saw she was sitting in the shade with a group of women. Peter Yoder's oldest daughter, a girl of eighteen, had both his babies in her arms.

"My wife tells me you have decided to let Maisie look after your children. What brought about your change of heart? The last time we spoke you said the two of you didn't get along. What's changed?"

Nathan wasn't surprised the news had gotten around so fast. He gave Gabe a wry smile. "I guess I have changed. You were right. The more I'm around Maisie, the more I can see that she is different from her sister."

"Things are better between the two of you, then?"

"We've found some common ground."

"Aha." Gabe grinned.

Nathan glanced at him. "What's that supposed to mean?"

"Nothing. It's just that I've noticed the way you look at her. And the way she looks at you."

"It's nothing like that. We both want the best for the babies. That's all."

"That's understandable. One more row of shingles and we're done. I'd better get a move on."

Nathan looked toward Maisie and met her gaze across the lawn. He raised his hand in a brief wave. She smiled softly and nodded to him, then looked away. There was nothing unusual in the exchange. What was Gabe seeing that Nathan didn't see?

"He's a handsome fella," Kathrine Yoder said with a giggle in her voice.

Maisie glanced at the cheerful teen. "Who is?"

"Nathan Weaver."

Maisie hoped she wasn't blushing. "He's well enough, I reckon."

"And hardworking, too. *Mamm* says that's the first thing a girl should look for in a man."

"Your mother is a wise woman. He's a little old for you, isn't he?" Maisie suggested.

"Oh, *ja*, but not for you."

"Me?" Maisie's voice squeaked in surprise.

"You can't stop looking at him except when he's looking this way," Bethany said.

Maisie looked around at the faces of the women she was sitting with. Bethany, Gemma, Dinah and Constance were all grinning at her. She was shocked. "*Nee*, you are mistaken. He's my brother-in-law."

"Was your brother-in-law," Constance said.

"There's nothing between us. I take care of his children. That's all there is."

"If you say so." Kathrine giggled again.

"I do," Maisie insisted. "I'm looking for my own place. Does anyone know of a small house or apartment that I can rent for a reasonable price?"

They all shook their heads, but then Bethany snapped her fingers. "I do. Your neighbor, Lilly Arnett, came in to have a clock fixed. She told Michael she had been thinking about taking in a renter at her place. She has an empty caretaker cottage or something. Do you know her?"

"I do. I'll talk to her. *Danki*."

"Its *goot* you are leaving Nathan's cabin," Constance said.

Maisie sobered. "I hope there hasn't been any gossip about us."

"Nothing like that," Constance assured her. She looked toward Nathan. "I was just thinking that absence makes the heart grow fonder."

Maisie didn't laugh as the other women did. Her absence from Nathan's house was the only hope she had to mend her heart, because being with him every day was breaking it in two.

Something was different about Maisie this morning.

Nathan couldn't put his finger on it, but something wasn't right.

She made a breakfast of dippy eggs, toast and oatmeal for him without comment. She fed the babies and dressed them in the new gowns she had sewn for them, while he ate instead of joining him. Not once did she meet his eyes.

As she was cleaning up, it struck him what was different. She wasn't humming or singing the way she normally did in the mornings.

"Are you feeling ill?" he asked.

"I'm fine." She kept her back to him as she worked at the sink.

He wanted to understand what was wrong. "Did the babies have a fussy night?"

"No more than usual. Are you going to be in here for a while?"

He had already finished his chores before breakfast and had even turned the cow and her new calf out into the pasture for the first time. "I reckon I can be."

"*Goot.* I'm going to go visit Lilly." She dried her hands, lifted her shawl off the peg near the door, flung it over her shoulders and went out.

"Beware of—" The door closed behind her before he could finish his warning. There had been occasional bear sightings in the area. He got up from the table. The dog was asleep under it. He nudged the hound with his toe. "Buddy, go outside with Annie."

Nathan winced and curled his fingers into fists. How long before Annie's name didn't roll off his lips? Not until her constant reminder lived somewhere else.

Buddy sat up. Nathan walked to the door and opened it. "Go keep an eye on Maisie."

The dog trotted out. The hound would alert her to any bear or moose in the area. Nathan closed the screen door behind the dog, leaving the wooden door open so he could enjoy the morning breeze. The air was distinctively cool. Summer was on the wane. Another month and he would be harvesting his potato crop. He wondered if Maisie would help or if he would need to hire someone. One of the Fisher brothers perhaps.

Gabe had it wrong about Nathan and Maisie. He wasn't interested in her romantically. When they weren't squabbling, she was fun to have around. She took wonderful care of the babies. He liked her cooking, but that wasn't the same as liking the woman.

Outside he heard Maisie shout followed by Buddy barking. He should see what was going on. Or maybe not. She had obviously wanted to get away from him. He cast a glance at the sleeping babies. Now was as good a time as any to get ready to go back to work on Monday. His chain saw needed sharpening. It was essential work. He headed to the barn to fetch it knowing the task was simply his excuse to check on Maisie.

He heard the cow bellowing loudly. Buddy's barking rose in volume. Nathan looked across the pasture. The cow was pacing frantically back and forth by the pond. He didn't see her calf. When she stepped far enough to one side, he saw Maisie up to her waist in the water with her arms around the calf's neck in the shallow end of the pond.

He vaulted the fence and hurried toward her. The cow decided he was an unwelcome intruder and tried to knock him aside. Buddy rushed in to nip her nose and distract her. "What are you doing?" he yelled at Maisie.

"There was a bear by the fence. I chased it off, but the calf became so frightened she ran into the pond. Now she is stuck in the mud."

Of course, Maisie would chase off a bear without calling for his help. His blood ran cold at the thought of how badly that could have ended. "I see she is stuck. Why are you in there?"

"She can't get out. I tried to free her, but it's no use. I'm afraid if I let go of her head she'll drown."

He started to wade toward Maisie, but quickly became mired in the mud himself. He stretched out his arm as far as he could. "Grab my hand."

She reached for him but her wet, muddy fingers slipped out of his grasp. The movement made her sink even farther. She shook her head. "Get back before you get stuck, too. We need a rope or a long branch."

"Hang on. I'll get something. Try not to struggle."

"That's what I keep telling this baby, but she won't listen." The calf continued thrashing her head back and forth, bawling pitifully for her mother. Her struggles were sending Maisie deeper into the mud.

Buddy was still doing his best to keep the

cow away. Nathan looked at Maisie. "If you can't save the calf, save yourself."

Maisie turned her face away from the splashing water the calf's movements sent flying. "Get a rope and save us both."

Nathan bolted for the barn. He grabbed a coil of rope from the tack room, opened the door to Donald's stall and led the big horse out into the pasture at a trot. At the edge of the pond, he quickly tied one end of the rope to Donald's halter and then waded toward Maisie. If he got stuck, the big horse could easily pull him free. The struggling calf had pushed her farther out. He paused with a coil in his hand. "Can you grab the rope if I throw it to you?"

"I'll try." She was up to her chest in the muddy water. He had no idea how deep the mud was where she was standing. If her legs were stuck, she wouldn't be able to swim.

He carefully tossed the rope toward her. She made a grab, but it floated beyond her reach. He quickly pulled it in and tried again. This time it landed across her arm. "I've got it," she shouted.

"Hold on and I'll pull you out." He started drawing the rope toward him.

"Let me get it around the calf first." The ensuing struggle had her up to her chin in the water. "Pull now," she said.

"Back, Donald. Back, back."

The big horse began walking backward until the rope was taut. Nathan kept pulling, too. The calf came slowly toward him and then popped up like a cork. He hauled it to shore as quickly as he could. Once the baby's legs touched dry ground, it collapsed in exhaustion. Nathan picked it up and carried it away from the shore so the heifer's mother could reach her. He hurried back to the water.

Maisie's pale face was barely above the surface. She held up one hand. "Hurry, Nathan."

He waded out until he was as close as he could get. It took him two tosses to get the rope near her hand. He started breathing again when she got hold of it. "Wrap it around your chest if you can, Annie."

She pulled the rope underwater. A few seconds later she gave a tiny nod. "Pull."

"Donald, back, back!"

The rope went tight, and her head went underwater. Nathan hauled on the rope, stepping even farther out and sinking above his knees in the muck. Suddenly she came up and slammed into his chest. He hung on to her as his horse dragged them both out of the water.

"Whoa, Donald. Whoa, boy," Nathan shouted from his back on the grass. The rope went slack. Donald walked up to sniff at Nathan. He reached up to rub the horse's nose. "*Goot* boy. Very *goot* boy."

He lay still for a few moments, relishing the weight of the woman in his arms. He could feel her rapid breathing. Her head was pressed against his chest. She must be able to hear the pounding of his heart. He looked down at her mud-covered face. "Are you hurt?"

"*Nee.*" She rolled to the side, sat up and began struggling to get the wet rope untied. He got to his feet. Suddenly he was furious with her for putting herself in such danger. "Annie Jean, that's the most foolish stunt you have ever pulled," he shouted, then realized his mistake.

Maisie surged to her feet, shimmied the rope to her ankles and kicked it aside as she glared at him. "I don't know how you could possibly know that, Nathan whatever-your-middle-name-is, since I am not *Annie*!"

She stormed past him, leaving a trail of dripping mud and water in her wake.

No, she was definitely not Annie.

"You're welcome," he shouted.

She stopped for a moment but then kept walking. He coiled up his rope, untied it from Donald's halter and led him to the barn. Nathan gave the horse an extra ration of oats and then followed Maisie to the house. The memory of the feel of her in his arms wouldn't fade.

He tried the door, but it was locked. He knocked. "Maisie, let me in. I'm sorry. It was the heat of the moment and her name just slipped out."

"Go away. I'm taking a bath."

He glanced along the porch and saw the galvanized tub still hanging on the wall. He unhooked it and knocked again.

"What?"

"Would you like to use the tub?" he asked, trying not to laugh. He was dripping wet and cold but he didn't care.

The door flew open. She had her *kapp* off. Her auburn hair hung down in long wet strands over her muddy dress and her eyes danced with green fire. *"Danki."* She pulled the tub from his hand and shut the door.

She opened it a second later. "And thanks for saving me and the calf." She closed the door before he could reply.

He looked down at his sopping clothes and knocked one more time. The door opened. A shirt followed by a pair of pants, a towel and a bar of soap came flying out. "Now go away," she shouted and slammed the door in his face.

Buddy came trotting up and scratched to be let in. Nathan looked at the dog. "I don't reckon she wants you right now. Might be for the best. She's touchy today."

Buddy scratched again. The door opened a crack. He wiggled inside before it shut.

Nathan picked up his dry clothes, the towel and the soap and headed to the pump to wash up in the cold water. No, she was definitely not Annie.

He had been angry because Maisie put herself in danger, but he realized how angry he still was with Annie. That feeling kept him from accepting Maisie as a person in her own right. Maybe it was time to let go of his bitterness.

After washing up and putting on dry clothes, Nathan walked up the rise to Annie's grave and squatted on his heels beside it. He saw the fresh flowers that had wilted and knew Maisie had put them there.

"I see your sister tends the dead as well as the living. Maisie is a born caretaker, but I reckon you knew that."

It felt odd but right to put his feelings into words.

"I'm at a loss, Annie. I'm angry. I'm sad. I'm bitter, but none of that affects you, does it? Only the living suffer. I've made Maisie's life miserable because she reminds me of you in so many ways, but I'm starting to see she isn't much like you at all. She's taking *goot* care of the babies. She has been showing me how to love them. How to give them more than food and shelter. If they learn to be caring people it will be because she has shown them how it's done. You were right to ask her to come."

He picked up a handful of dirt and let it trickle through his fingers. "You hurt me, Annie. You broke my heart, made me doubt myself. You caused me to shut myself away from my faith and those who would help me. I'm never going to know why, am I?"

He rose to his feet and slipped his hands in his pockets. "The bishop here said forgiveness must come first, even before understanding. That's a hard thing to wrap my brain around. I wanted answers before I forgave you, but I'll never have them. I can't live my life with this weight on my soul. Those around me deserve better."

He wiped at the wetness on his cheeks. "So I forgive you, *liebling*. Rest in peace."

He turned away and walked down the hill with a lightness in his heart that he hadn't known for nearly a year. At last, he was free.

Maisie washed the muck and pond smell from her long hair at the kitchen sink with cold water while she waited for her bath water to heat up. She had every pot full of water and the stove on high.

She shouldn't be this upset. Nathan hadn't meant to call her by Annie's name, but it hurt, anyway. Closing her eyes, she faced her sad desire. She wanted to be back in Nathan's arms just for a moment. Even if they were both exhausted and soaking wet in smelly pond water. She chased the image from her mind. Had he been holding her? Or had he been holding Annie?

She wanted his concern to be for her, but she would never be sure if he was thinking about her or if he was thinking about her sister.

She wasn't going to ask him. She wasn't going to beg for his attention the way she had begged for John's in a hopeless effort to make her marriage into something it hadn't been.

What she needed was to get away. Not from the babies, but from Nathan. She needed her own place, where she didn't have to hide her feelings. She could pretend for the few minutes that they would meet each day that she was fine.

She took a quick bath in lukewarm water because she was too impatient to wait for the water to get hot. She would go see Lilly today. She prayed her friend hadn't already rented the little ivy-covered cottage. It would be perfect for her and the babies and close enough to the cabin to make it easy for her to share their care with Nathan.

She dried off, emptied out the tub and took her clothing out to the washing machine. She saw Nathan's clothes piled on a chair beside the washer. She tossed everything in together and went back to clean up her mess in the kitchen. She had no choice but to wear her hair down. It wouldn't dry if she put it up or braided it. She used a kerchief to cover her head and tied it at the nape of her neck. Then she went to the front door, took a deep breath and stepped out. Nathan was waiting on the steps.

His uncertain smile made her traitorous heart turn over in her chest. Why was she falling in love with a man who couldn't care for her because of how she looked? She put her shoulders back, determined to go through with her plan. "Would you bring the buggy around, please? I'm taking the babies to visit Lilly. She hasn't seen them yet."

"Are you okay?"

"Of course I am. Why wouldn't I be?"

She was embarrassed to have him see her hair hanging down her back. A woman's hair was her crowning glory, to be viewed only by God and her husband.

"I was afraid the rope might have hurt your skin."

"I'll have a bruise or two, but otherwise I'm fine. The buggy, please?" She turned on her heel and went back inside before he could ask her anything else. She put the babies in their carriers and waited outside until Nathan brought Sassy and the buggy around. She got in and picked up the lines. "I'm not sure when I'll be back."

She put Sassy into a quick trot. The sooner she was away from Nathan, the sooner she could gather her scattered wits and decide what to do next.

Chapter Thirteen

Nathan heard a horse and buggy a short time later and wondered if Maisie was returning already. He put down the harness he was cleaning and opened his door. He was surprised to see the bishop step out of the buggy.

Nathan pulled his door shut and started walking toward him. "Good day, Bishop Schultz. What can I do for you?"

The bishop turned around and smiled. "I came to see how you are getting along, brother."

"Well enough." Nathan nodded toward the barn. "I have coffee down in my room if you'd like some."

The bishop looked puzzled. "In your room?"

"I sleep down there. That gives Maisie and the babies more room in the cabin."

The bishop's eyes widened. "Of course."

Nathan suddenly felt self-conscious about

the arrangement. "Come in. Maisie and the children have gone to visit Lilly Arnett." Nathan walked ahead of Bishop Schultz and opened the cabin door.

The bishop stopped on the porch to look the building over. "I understand you built this place yourself."

"With my team and an occasional hand from the men I work with at the lumber camp."

"It looks solid."

"The first winter will be the real test. Nothing like a wind-driven snow to find the cracks and poor joints." Nathan walked inside, hung his hat on a peg and indicated his chair. "Have a seat."

The bishop hung up his own hat. "Show me around first. I see you have a loft. How wide is this place?"

"Twenty feet."

He walked to the center of the room and turned around. "And how long?"

"Thirty-five feet."

"And could you make it smaller?"

"Smaller is easier than making it bigger. Why?"

"The *Englisch* are looking for smaller homes now. They call them tiny houses. I have built a few and they have sold well. I think there is a certain appeal to a log home, especially here in Maine. How long would it take you to construct one that was twelve feet wide and, say, twenty feet long with a loft like this one?"

"It would depend on the weather and if the materials were readily available. In the right conditions, I think eight weeks for the shell."

"It's an interesting thought." He turned to Nathan. "But not why I am here today."

Nathan sat on the sofa and waited until the bishop took a seat. "Why have you come?"

"I haven't found anyone to work for you, I'm sorry to say. I heard that your last candidate wasn't suitable."

"Maisie did not think so, but I took your advice and asked her to care for the babies as their *kinder heeda*."

"She has invested her heart in her sister's children, hasn't she?"

Nathan leaned back. "That she has."

"And how are the two of you getting along?"

"Fine. She takes good care of my home. She's a fine cook. She keeps an eye on my livestock, too." Nathan grinned at the memory of Maisie up to her neck in muddy water.

The bishop was watching him intently. "So you get on well?"

"I would say so. I try not to be irritated and she tries not to be aggravating for the most part."

"Worthy goals. And you find her trustworthy?"

"I would not leave my children in her care if I didn't."

"Is she a devout woman of faith? Will she instill a love of *Gott* in the children?"

"Absolutely. Her faith is rock-solid." And stronger than Nathan's, but he knew his faith could grow and flourish now.

"That's reassuring to hear from someone who knows her best. We didn't have a chance to talk much at your wife's funeral. I could see that you weren't ready. You did say that she had left you and you didn't know where she was until I brought you the news of her death."

Nathan leaned forward and clasped his hands together, propping his elbows on his knees. "That's right. She left me with only a note. I didn't know I had children until you came that day."

"When was the last time you saw Annie?"

"Last December. Two months after our wedding."

"You grieved the loss of her then, didn't you?"

"I guess I did. Except I held on to a small measure of hope that she would return."

"That's understandable. It's what any man would want. I ask because what I'm about to suggest may seem unusual. Especially to those who don't know your story."

Nathan didn't understand. "Unusual how?"

"Your children are going to need more than a nanny. They're going to need a mother. Have you considered remarrying?"

Nathan held up one hand in surprise. "*Nee*, I'm not ready to look for a wife."

Would he ever be ready to trust his heart to another woman? It was hard to imagine.

"A broken heart is sometimes slow to heal," the bishop said. "But not every marriage is based on romantic love. A marriage can be successful if it is based on love of *Gott*, mutual respect and shared goals. Love between two people can grow out of friendship over time. There are several young women in our community who would make wonderful mothers for your children, but I think you already know the best candidate."

Nathan shook his head. "I don't know who you're talking about."

The bishop arched an eyebrow. "I think you do. Maisie."

Nathan was thunderstruck. "Maisie? You think I should marry Maisie?"

"I am not in the habit of playing matchmaker. That is something my wife enjoys. It was her suggestion that I speak to you on the subject."

This was unbelievable. Nathan got to his feet, walked to the door and opened it. "Please, tell your wife I appreciate her concern, but I have no intention of taking a wife. Especially not Maisie."

The bishop rose, walked over to get his hat and stopped beside Nathan. "I will tell her what you said, but she's going to ask me why 'especially' not Maisie?"

"She's too much like Annie."

"Your own words belie that. You said she keeps a fine home, loves the babies, she's a devout member of our faith, she's even a good cook. Which of those qualities are too much like those of the wife who broke her vows and abandoned you?"

Nathan clenched his jaw so hard his teeth ached. The man didn't understand. "Good day, Bishop. It was kind of you to call," he said when he had his temper under control.

The bishop tried to hold back a smile. "I found it very enlightening myself." He nodded to Nathan and went to his buggy.

Nathan shut the door and leaned against it with both hands. "Of all the ridiculous, unbelievable, preposterous ideas. Me? Marry

Maisie?" What was the man thinking? Of course, she was like her sister. They're twins.

He remembered Maisie's furious face when she'd shouted, "I am not Annie."

His anger faded. She wasn't Annie. Annie hadn't had a temper. Annie never sang in the mornings. She never suggested that he read from the Bible in the evenings or enjoyed visiting with friends. She told Nathan that he was enough for her, but she had broken the vows she made before God and their community.

He forgave Annie, but that didn't mean he could forget what she had done or want to replace her. The children had Maisie and they had him when he could be with them. That would be enough.

Besides, Maisie would laugh at the suggestion of marrying him.

Wouldn't she?

It didn't matter. He wasn't about to ask her.

Grabbing his hat, he went out and headed down the lane. He had told the Fisher men that he'd be out to look at their trees to see if they had enough harvestable wood to build an addition on Gabe's shop. Now was as good a time as any and he could use the long walk.

Lilly came out to greet Maisie as soon as she stopped Sassy outside the front gate. "Maisie, how wonderful to see you again. Do come in. I just took some banana bread out of the oven."

Seeing the welcome in Lilly's eyes made Maisie feel better. "I'm glad you're home. I have brought some visitors with me."

Lilly's expression brightened even more. "The babies? Oh, how wonderful. Bring them inside. Will your horse be okay out here by herself?"

"She'll be fine. Give me a hand with these chubby children. I can't believe how much weight they have put on since I first arrived. These little baskets won't hold them much longer."

She handed Charity to Lilly and got out with Jacob. Lilly was smiling tenderly at the little girl. "She certainly looks like you."

"She looks like her mother."

Lilly immediately appeared contrite. "I'm sorry. That was thoughtless of me."

"It's okay. If she looks like her mother she has to look like me, too."

"My gracious, woman, look at all your hair."

Maisie blushed. "I hope you don't mind my wearing it down. I washed it and I'm waiting for it to dry."

"I don't mind at all. It's a beautiful auburn color. I shouldn't say that, should I? The Amish don't want to be called handsome or beautiful. They want to be plain."

"Because it isn't our outward looks that please God."

"That is so true. Well, come in. I want to hold that little boy, too."

Maisie followed her into the kitchen, which had bold yellow stripes on the walls, white cupboards with yellow daisy-shaped pulls and numerous paintings and sketches of different flowers on the walls. "Your kitchen is colorful."

"I know it must seem gaudy to you, but I like it." She placed Charity's basket on one of the white wooden chairs.

"Did you do the paintings?" Maisie asked, impressed with the quality of them.

"Most of them I purchased from local artists. Several of them I got from Esther Fisher. Gabe's wife. She and I share a love of wildflowers. I like to grow them. She likes to sketch and paint them. How is Nathan?" Lilly asked, suddenly serious.

"As well as can be expected." Maisie concentrated on lifting Jacob out of his basket. She handed him to Lilly, who took him tenderly. Talking about Nathan was the last thing she wanted to do.

Lilly smiled at the babe in her arms. "It's

been ages since I've held a newborn. You forget how tiny they are. What a perfectly wonderful way God chose to start a person."

"They certainly have their own personalities already. The reason I came today was because I heard you are renting out your cottage. I'm looking for a place and it would be close to Nathan's."

Lilly's face fell. "Oh, no. I wish I had known."

"You've already rented it to someone else?" Maisie struggled to hide her disappointment.

"I'm afraid so. Mr. Meriwether knows a gentleman from Philadelphia who is looking for a weekend getaway home. He's going to take it. I'm so sorry."

It had been too good to be true. Maisie managed to smile. "All things are as God wills. I'll keep looking. If you hear of anything, please let me know."

"I will. Now can I interest you in a slice of banana bread and some milk?"

Maisie nodded. "That sounds wonderful."

"Let's have it out on the patio so the sun can dry your hair."

Maisie enjoyed Lilly's treat and her company for another hour while Lilly admired the babies, but Maisie knew she was simply putting off her return to Nathan's cabin. What could she say to explain her outburst over something as simple as being called the wrong name? She couldn't tell him the truth. That she was falling in love with him and she wanted him to care for her, not her sister.

Nathan wasn't home when Maisie returned. She was glad of the reprieve but knew it was only that. She stabled Sassy and took the babies inside. They weren't ready for their feedings, so she settled them in their cradles and fixed a roast with new potatoes and carrots from the garden and put it in the oven. She had time to make a salad of fresh greens to go with the roast before Jacob began fussing.

She fixed his bottle and settled in the rocker with him. "I'm beginning to think Agnes Martin was right about us. You demand attention and I jump to take care of you. I think I'm spoiling you." She bent to kiss his forehead. When she looked up, Nathan was watching her from the doorway.

Nathan stared at Maisie as if seeing her for the first time. It wasn't her resemblance to Annie that caught and held his attention. It was a look of love in her eyes when she gazed at his son. He didn't know it at the time, but this was why he had built this cabin. To someday see a gentle, sweet woman rocking his baby by his hearth.

A sense of wonder filled him. This is what he wanted, what he had always wanted—a family of his own.

How could he have been so blind as to see only Annie when he looked at Maisie? Their similarities were minor things. It was Maisie's inner beauty that filled his heart with happiness. This felt like coming home.

He was afraid if he spoke that feeling would vanish, but he couldn't stand in the door all night. "Did Lilly enjoy meeting our *kinder*?"

"She did. I had a hard time prying them out of her arms. Nathan, about before—"

"Forget it. I have."

"I was very rude to you and I'm sorry."

"Nothing to be sorry for." He picked up Charity and sat in his chair. "Aggravating and irritated, I reckon we'll do that to each other now and again. It doesn't matter as long as we share this quiet joy together."

She smiled softly. "They are a blessing, to be sure. Where were you this evening, if you don't mind my asking?"

"I walked over to the Fisher place to look through their forests and see if they have enough usable timber to build a log addition on Gabe's shop."

"Do they?"

"They do, but some of it is going to be hard

to reach with heavy equipment, which I'm guessing is why the bigger trees haven't been cut already."

"What about using horses?"

"It is certainly possible. It would take a little longer but the impact on the land would be a lot less. In fact, they offered me the job."

Her bright smile did funny things to his stomach. "Are you going to take it? What about the lumber camp?"

He studied Charity's face as he stroked her cheek. She turned her mouth toward his finger and opened her lips. "I would still need to work for Davis. This would be a side job. I think this little girl is ready to eat."

"Her bottle is warming on the stove."

He got up to get it.

"I went to see Lilly because I heard she had a place to rent," Maisie said.

He froze. They had talked about her getting her own place, but he didn't think it would be so soon. "It would be close."

"Someone else had rented it before I got there."

His relief was startling. She wasn't leaving him yet. "I hope you know there's no rush. I'm perfectly comfortable where I am."

"I appreciate you saying that, but I do feel

odd sleeping in your bed while you sleep in the barn."

He returned to his chair with the warm bottle of milk, picked up his daughter and began to feed her. "In that case, we can trade beds. You can have the cot up there and I'll haul the big bed down to my room."

Maisie laughed. "There isn't enough space in there. You would have to walk sideways to get to the stove."

"That's true. I guess you're stuck with the better bed."

"You could move Mack to your room and put the bed in his stall. There'd be plenty of room then."

He laughed. "No way. Donald snores. I'm not sleeping next to him."

She grinned. "I guess it would make the cow and her calf jealous if Mack had a stove and they didn't."

He tried to sound serious. "We could have a barnyard revolt on our hands before we know it."

"The roosters might start crowing at midnight in protest."

He smacked his hand on the arm of his chair. "That settles it. Mack is staying in his old stall no matter how upset he gets."

She giggled and he loved the sound. It was

good to see her being carefree, even for a little while.

"Both babies are awake and not crying. You should read to them," she said.

"Why don't you sing instead? There is a lullaby my *mamm* used to sing to me. *'Schloof, Bobbeli, Schloof'*—do you know it?"

"'Sleep, Baby, Sleep.' Of course I know it. I've sung it many times." She put her head back in the chair and began to sing softly. He joined in and their voices blended in a pleasant harmony. By the time the song ended, both babies were sleeping. She put Jacob to bed and then took Charity from Nathan's arms and tucked her in.

He leaned back in his chair and glanced toward the kitchen. "Something sure smells *goot*. What's for supper?"

"Is food all you think about?" she asked, still smiling.

"I reckon," he replied, but it wasn't true.

He was thinking about the reason for the bishop's visit. Marriage. Maybe it wasn't such a far-fetched idea after all. There would be advantages to a more permanent relationship.

But could he get Maisie to see them?

Their relationship had been rocky at best. Only when they were with the children did they seem of one accord. He couldn't do much to improve the situation unless he was home.

He got out of his chair. "I'm going down to the phone. I should leave a message saying the nanny position has been filled in case anyone calls about it."

"Okay, I'll wait supper on you."

"Danki."

He got his hat and went out. When he reached the phone booth, he recorded a new message and then dialed the number for his boss.

Maisie followed the smell of frying bacon down to the kitchen early the next morning. Nathan stood in front of the stove with a large blue apron over his clothing.

"What are you doing?" she asked.

He turned to her with a breathtaking smile. "I thought I would make breakfast for a change. I hope you like hearty eggs."

This was different. "And what are hearty eggs?"

"Eggs with diced onions, grated cheese, grated potatoes, crumbled bacon and hot sauce to top it off. One of the guys at the lumber camp showed me how to make them."

"That all sounds fine except for the hot sauce. Is it optional?" she asked hopefully.

"Of course, but you'll never know if you like something new unless you try it."

She was almost convinced but thought better of it. "I'll have mine less hearty than yours."

"Don't tell me you're a fraidy-cat." He shook his head and make a tsking sound. He brought the plate to the table and sat down.

After saying grace, she cautiously tried a spoonful and found it was quite good. He pushed the hot sauce toward her.

She sprinkled a few drops on her next spoonful and regretted it as soon as it touched her tongue. With her mouth open, she tried to fan the heat away. "Water," she croaked.

He put a glass of milk in front of her. "This is better."

She didn't care what it was as long as it was liquid. After several moments, the heat died away. She frowned at him. "Why would anyone want to eat something painful?"

"It wasn't that bad. Admit it."

"I admit nothing. I believe I'll have some toast."

He pushed the plate where she could reach it. "The Fishers are hosting a frolic on Thursday to build a greenhouse. I thought you might want to go."

"I'll see. It depends on the babies and if I

feel up to it. It's a pity you can't go. I know you've become friends with Gabe."

"Who says I'm not going?"

She frowned. "What about your work?"

"I told you Davis hired another feller. I called him last night and asked to use the rest of the time off he'd promised me when I told him about Annie and the babies. He agreed."

"But what about your pay?"

"I'm not getting paid time off, but I can cut and haul the timber for Zeke Fisher and make up the difference. I want some time with you and the babies before you get your own place. Last night was nice, wasn't it?"

Smiling at the memory, she nodded. "It was a pleasant evening." Following a stressful day.

"*Goot.* We should have more like that one." He winked at her. Actually winked. "Without the squabbling first, *ja*?"

Chapter Fourteen

❧

Maisie poured coffee refills into the cups for her guests. "Have either of you heard about a place for rent nearby?" Bethany and Gemma had surprised her with a visit on Thursday morning.

Both women shook their heads. "How are you and Nathan getting along?" Bethany asked.

Maisie grinned. "The change has been like night and day. I don't know what happened. Well, maybe I do. I gave him a frightful scolding last Sunday. Nathan has been so nice to me these past few days that I'm tempted to scold him once a week."

"That's what I do to Jesse," Gemma said, hiding a smile with her cup. Since Jesse towered over little Gemma, the thought of her shaking her finger at her mountain of a husband made both Bethany and Maisie chuckle.

Gemma leaned forward. "Did Agnes Martin really apply for the babysitting job?"

Maisie nodded. "I'm sure she's a nice woman but she didn't seem a good fit for the twins."

"You made a wise choice," Gemma said, sharing a speaking glance with Bethany.

"Agnes wanted Gemma to be shunned when she first returned to us," Bethany said. "After the bishop had granted her forgiveness."

"I was pregnant but not yet married," Gemma explained shyly.

"Agnes isn't the kindest soul," Bethany said. "I don't think she would have been right for the job."

Maisie shook her head. "You should have met the *Englisch* woman who came with her résumé. She couldn't stop checking her phone the entire time I was talking to her. I was shocked. Who would hire someone like that to watch their children?"

"Nathan chose the right woman when he chose you," Bethany said. "We can all see how much you love those babies. They will never know another mother except you."

"Unless Nathan remarries," Maisie said quietly. Neither of her friends said anything.

Maisie pasted a smile on her face. "Are you going to the frolic at the Fishers' today?"

"I wouldn't miss it." Bethany set her cup in the saucer. "I made a cherry pie for dessert. What about you, Maisie, what are you bringing?"

"Nathan said he likes apple. I think I'll make two of those. One for the frolic and one to leave here."

Bethany rolled her eyes. "I hope he knows how fortunate he is to get a *kinder heeda* who cooks and cleans, too."

"We should get going," Gemma said. "Jesse loves watching the children for me but for some reason the house is always a mess when I get back. We'll see you this afternoon."

As much as she enjoyed their company, Maisie was glad to see them on their way. She had pies to make because she knew Nathan would enjoy them. He loved the smell of something good cooking in the kitchen and she liked doing it. It was a small thing, but it made her happy to make him happy.

Until she found a place of her own, she reminded herself. And then he would be cooking for himself again unless she took pity on him and cooked something while he was at work. It was getting harder to contemplate making that break from him. His recent kindness had her puzzled, but perhaps he realized how unfair he'd been to her in those first few weeks.

She wanted to think they could come out of this as friends.

Nathan paced in his small room as he tried to decide what to say to Maisie. He was going to propose today. Things had been good between them since Sunday. He was afraid if he waited any longer something would happen to derail his plans.

Her friends had left nearly ten minutes ago. If he waited much longer his courage was going to fail him.

He left the barn and walked up to the house. Outside the door, he stopped to take several deep breaths.

This was a good idea. He'd thought it through carefully so why was his stomach churning?

It was the logical thing to do. Maisie would understand and appreciate the advantages when he pointed them out. She wasn't the most logical of women—he'd seen that—but she had a good head on her shoulders when she wasn't angry. He was sure that she had gotten past being upset with him.

Nathan rubbed his suddenly sweaty palms on the sides of his pants. This was as good a time as any. He opened the door and stepped in the house.

She was in the kitchen slicing apples into a clear bowl with cinnamon and sugar. Two pie pans with unbaked crusts were sitting on the table. He walked up beside her and leaned against the counter. He crossed his arms because he didn't know what to do with his hands.

He cleared his throat. "Making apple pies?"

A smile twitched the corners of her lips. "What gave me away?"

"Yeah. It's pretty obvious." For some reason the collar of his shirt suddenly seemed too tight. He gave a small tug on it.

"Did you want something?" she asked, reaching for another apple in the bowl beside her. She deftly peeled it and started slicing until only the core was left. She tossed it in the garbage can beside her.

"There's something I'd like to talk to you about. I think you'll see that it's also an obvious solution." Did he tell her it was the bishop's suggestion? He decided not to mention that.

"So talk." She reached for another apple.

His hand shot out to cover hers. "Could you stop doing that for a minute?" Her hand was so small and soft compared to his. A tingle skittered up his arm, centered in his chest and made his breath catch in his throat. He jerked his hand away.

A tiny frown creased her brow as she looked at him. "I have to get these in the oven if they are going to be done in time for the frolic."

"This won't take long."

She laid the knife on the counter and dried her hands on her apron. "You have my attention. What is it?"

"I've been thinking about our situation." He swallowed hard. Was it hot in here? From the stove. Of course.

"And?"

"I have a solution. Please hear me out."

She crossed her arms. Her eyes narrowed slightly. He could still see the gold flecks in her green irises. He hadn't noticed before what thick eyelashes she had and how they framed her eyes so beautifully.

"Do I have something on my face?" She rubbed her cheek.

"Nee." Should he tell her that she had beautiful eyes? Maybe not. It had nothing to do with their situation. He needed to ease into this conversation, point out the advantages for her.

She tapped one foot. "I'm waiting."

"You have pretty eyes."

A blush crept up her cheeks. "That's kind of you to say. Is there anything else?"

"I think we should get married."

Her eyes widened with shock. "What?"

"There are so many advantages," he said quickly. "You won't have to look for a place to live. You can live here. We can live here. You won't just be a nanny to the children—you'll be their mother. I know you would like that. You would never have to be parted from them. I know you already feel in your heart that they are yours."

She half turned away from him and braced her hands on the counter. "I do love them. What about us?"

"Us?"

"*Ja*, us. As in you and me. Together."

Why was she making this so hard? A simple *yes* was enough.

All the things he wanted to say ran through his mind.

Marry me so I can take you in my arms and kiss you. Let me hold you close and tell you my hopes and my dreams and hear you whisper that you understand. That you care for me.

He would say those things in time, but he wasn't sure she was ready to hear them. "We get along pretty well now. You have a bit of a temper, but you also have a generous heart. I don't see a reason it won't work." He stared at his toes. "I wouldn't make any demands on you," he said softly.

She was silent for several long, uneasy moments. He saw her fingers splayed on the counter curl into her palms and then slowly open again. She drew a deep breath. "Getting my own place is a better idea."

He jerked upright. "But I thought you liked it here. You have ideas for how to make the cabin a better home. You are going to expand the garden."

She picked up her knife again. "I have to finish these. We don't want to be late."

"You don't want to marry me?"

"Nee."

Why did that one word hurt so much? He had trouble drawing his next breath. What else could he have said? What could he offer her? Maybe he was rushing her. "If you want to think it over, I don't have to have an answer right now."

She whirled to face him. "I'm not a replacement for my sister. I'm a person with my own thoughts and my own feelings. Did you really expect me to jump into your arms and be thrilled at the idea of stepping into my dead sister's shoes?"

"That wasn't what I was thinking. Look, I have rushed you. I'm sorry. Take some time and think it over. I believe you'll see it's best for both of us and the babies."

"You have my answer. Now please get out of the kitchen and let me finish these pies." Her voice broke and she threw the apple core into the trash hard enough to make it bounce out and land at his feet.

Nathan let his hands drop to his sides. She didn't want him. Just like her sister hadn't wanted him. A sick feeling seeped through his body. What was wrong with him? Why wouldn't she give him a chance to make it work between them?

It didn't matter. He could see her mind was made up. "Fine. Call me when you're ready to leave. I'll be in the barn."

He stormed out of the kitchen and slammed the door, wishing he could somehow leave the pain behind, too, but it stayed like a ball of broken glass in the center of his chest.

Maisie covered her face with her hands as her sobs broke free. She sank to the floor in a heap of misery as hot tears flowed down her cheeks. He had ruined everything. She couldn't pretend that he was starting to like her. He had only been nice because he thought that would persuade her to accept his proposal. He could bring himself to marry her, but he didn't love her. He couldn't say the words she needed to hear. She was a solution to his problem. Not someone he loved. She cried until there were no tears left and then she hauled herself to her feet and washed her face at the sink.

God forgive her, she had almost said yes. She loved him. He had offered her everything she wanted except the one thing she could never have. His heart. Annie had ruined him more completely than she could have known.

As much as Maisie had grown to love Nathan, she knew she couldn't fix him. Couldn't change him. She had tried with John and only earned more heartache.

She was greedy. She wanted more. She wanted to be loved because she was Maisie. Nathan would never see her as anything but a pale imitation of Annie.

The magnitude of Maisie's grief hollowed out a place where her heart should have been. She wouldn't be able to stay here. Constance had offered to let her live with them. That's what she would do. Nathan was going to be off work for several weeks. The babies would be fine with him, though the thought of leaving them was unbearable. She needed time to decide what to do next.

She wouldn't be able to look at Nathan every

day and know she could have been his wife if she had been willing to accept his proposal.

It wasn't fair. She had already endured one loveless marriage. She would not subject herself to that humiliation again.

Nathan hit the nail with as much force as he could muster. The head of his hammer slipped off and the nail bent. It was too far in to be pulled out so he hit it over and over until he smashed the bent part into the wood.

"What did that poor nail ever do to you?" Gabe asked from his position a few rafters over.

"It's not the nail," Nathan grumbled.

"Oh, it's the woman." Gabe chuckled.

"What are you laughing at?"

"I've been where you are and I'm happy to say I got through it."

"I asked Maisie to marry me."

"Did you? That's a surprise. What did she say? I ask, although I think I already know the answer."

"I don't understand the woman. I offered her everything that I have. Everything she wants and she still said no."

"That was going to be my guess. Maybe she is in love with someone else," Gabe suggested.

Nathan scoffed at the idea. "If I thought that I wouldn't have asked her to marry me."

Gabe drove in his nail then slipped his hammer into the loop on his tool belt. "I don't know what to say. When a man tells a woman that he loves her, he expects her to feel the same and sometimes it doesn't happen that way."

"I didn't say that."

"You didn't what?"

"I didn't tell her that I love her."

"Okay. That might have been your first mistake." Gabe scratched the side of his head. "You asked a woman you're not in love with to marry you?"

"I didn't know I was in love with her. I thought I admired her. I respected her. I thought she'd make the perfect mother. It didn't hit me just how much I needed her until she said no."

"You didn't know you were in love with her then, but you do now?"

"Of course, I'm in love with Maisie. She's everything I need. She's as wonderful and spectacular as her name."

"So why can't you tell her that?"

Nathan drove in the next nail, then he looked at his friend. "Because she won't believe me. She thinks I'm still in love with her sister. She thinks I see her as a substitute for the wife I lost."

"And why would she think that?"

Nathan hung his head. "Because that was what I saw when she first arrived. I couldn't bear to look at Maisie because I saw Annie."

"Let me guess. You may have mentioned that to her at some point."

"So now you see why I can't just tell her that my feelings have changed and that I love her for who she is and not because she looks like my dead wife."

"You have a problem, Nathan."

"Tell me something I don't know." He hammered in another nail.

"Well, you're a fool for one thing."

Nathan shot him a sour look. "That didn't help."

"If she thinks you only see Annie when you look at her then you have to convince her otherwise."

"It's too late for that. She is willing to take care of the babies while I'm at work but otherwise we won't see each other."

"Ours is a small community. You will have to see each other at church services and gatherings."

"I know, I know. I'll see her every day when

she comes to stay with the children. I don't know how I'm going to endure that. I don't want to take them away from her. She loves them as much as I do."

"Then perhaps you should let her raise the children."

Nathan jerked upright. "I'm not going to give away my flesh and blood. I want my family with me. I'm not going to abandon them."

"Then you'll have to convince Maisie that you see her and not her sister."

"Any suggestions on how I do that?"

"Pray about it. God is all-knowing. He has the answers if you're willing to listen."

Gabe got down, leaving Nathan to wonder if God would listen to a man who had turned his back on Him and was only now stumbling back into his faith.

Maisie brought out a plate of fried chicken and set it on the table already overloaded with food. Constance came out and rang the dinner bell. Maisie shaded her eyes with her hand and looked toward the building site. All the men wore the same clothing—the same dark blue pants with suspenders and light blue shirts— but she didn't have any trouble picking out Nathan. Her heart foolishly ached at the sight of him. He was on the rafters. He left off working along with the others as they all made their way toward the food.

Would she ever be able to look at him without wanting to be in his arms?

She moved her plate of chicken over and pulled a bowl of baked beans next to it. A second later, she moved them back. Then she stood staring at them.

"What's the matter with you?" Gemma asked, setting a bowl of coleslaw beside the baked beans.

"Nothing. Why do you ask?"

"Because you've been staring at your plate of chicken for a long time. Is there something wrong with it?"

"Everything is wrong with it." Tears sprang to Maisie's eyes. She covered her face with her hands and started crying.

She felt Gemma take her arm. "I don't think this is a conversation your chicken should overhear. Come with me."

Maisie allowed Gemma to lead her around to the other side of the house and into the garden. Gemma sat down on a wooden bench and pulled Maisie down beside her. "Okay, I know it wasn't about the food. What's really bothering you?"

Maisie looked into Gemma's sympathetic eyes and blurted out the truth. "Nathan has asked me to marry him."

"That's wonderful news."

Maisie shook her head. "No, it isn't."

Gemma became instantly sympathetic. "Oh. You don't love him. How awkward for you."

"I love him. I love him with all my heart."

Gemma took Maisie's hand and patted it. "I'm missing something. You love Nathan and he has asked you to marry him, but that isn't good news?"

"Don't you see?"

"Not right this minute. Perhaps you could explain."

Maisie shook her head. "Nathan said he could give me a home. I could help him raise the children. I'd never have to be parted from them."

"It sounds wonderful. What did he miss?"

"The one thing he can't give me. Love. He didn't say that he loved me. Nathan is still in love with Annie. He sees me as a replacement for her. Not an original but almost as good. Sometimes he even calls me by her name." She jumped to her feet and began to pace among the flowers.

Gemma followed Maisie and put an arm

around her shoulders. "Now I understand. So you turned him down, didn't you?"

"Of course I did. I deserve to be loved because I am who *Gott* made me. I'm not an Annie replacement."

"What will you do now?"

"Stay with Constance and the bishop, I guess, but I don't want to leave my babies." Her voice broke. "I love them more than my own life. They are part of my heart and soul. I don't know what to do."

"Our Lord will find a way through this for you. You must have faith. In the meantime you can stay with Jesse and me."

"*Danki*, but I need to be with the children. Can someone take us home?"

"Certainly. Jesse will take you."

"If anyone is going to take my family home it will be me," Nathan said. He was standing at the side of the house with his hands clenched into fists.

How much had he heard? Maisie turned away.

"I'm going to go help serve the food," Gemma said brightly.

"Don't go," Maisie begged, reaching for her friend.

"You don't need me, and Nathan would rather I left, wouldn't you?"

"Jesse married a smart woman."

"I tell him that all the time." Gemma gave Nathan's arm a squeeze and walked around him.

"You and I need to have another conversation," Nathan said. "Do you want to do it here or shall we go home, where we won't be interrupted?"

"I don't know what else there is to say."

"A lot, actually. Things I should have said before. Things I didn't know I needed to say."

She didn't want to rehash her heartache, but she saw the determination in his face and nodded. It was better to be humiliated in private. "I'll get the babies."

Chapter Fifteen

❧

The silence in the buggy during the ride back to the cabin was stifling. Even the babies seemed to pick up on the tension. They whimpered and squirmed in their baskets. Maisie kept rocking them, trying to reassure them, but it didn't help. She dreaded what she knew was to come but she was thankful when he turned into his lane. It was better to get it over with sooner rather than later.

When they drove into the yard, she saw there was a dark gray car sitting beside the house. Maisie didn't see anyone around. She looked at Nathan. "Do you recognize the car? Is it one of your logging friends?"

"It looks too high-dollar for the lumberjacks I know." He got out and came around to open Maisie's door.

She handed out the twins in their baskets

and noticed movement up on the rise near Annie's grave. A man was kneeling by the marker. It was Gavin Porter.

"It's someone Annie and I used to know. I'll go talk to him," she said.

"You and I need to talk."

"We will." She clasped her hands together tightly as she stared up the hill.

"Do you want me to come with you?" Nathan asked softly.

If what she suspected was true, Nathan deserved to hear it firsthand. She nodded. "I think you should."

Maisie walked slowly up the rise and stopped a few feet away from the kneeling figure. "Hello, Gavin. I'm sorry we weren't here to greet you."

He stared at the small white cross bearing Annie's name. "I'm sorry for a lot of things."

He got to his feet and faced them. "Hello, Maisie, and you must be Nathan."

"I am." Nathan eyed him suspiciously.

"And these are Annie's babies?" Gavin smiled at the carriers. "May I see them?"

Nathan laid the baskets in the grass and opened them wide enough for him to peer in.

"Charity and Jacob," Maisie said. "I wrote to your parents to let them know about Annie's passing, but I didn't know how to contact you."

"They called me. I wish things had turned out differently." He glanced back at the grave. "She was the light of my life."

"She was with you, then?" Maisie folded her arms and looked down. "I wondered as much, but when your parents didn't know where she was I thought I must be mistaken."

Nathan scowled. "Annie left me to be with you?"

"We fell in love when she worked for my family, but I was married to a dying woman. After my wife passed away, I didn't think I had the right to ask Annie to choose between me and her faith. So I moved to New York with the kids. I thought I could start a new life, but all I could think about was how much I missed her. I wrote to her and asked her to come be with me and the children. I didn't know she had gotten married or I never would have asked. When she told me, I was shocked, but I didn't want to lose her again." His expression was so earnest that Maisie believed him.

She took hold of Nathan's arm. This had to be so painful for him. "Why the secrecy, Gavin?" she asked. "Why not let your parents or me know that she was with you?"

"Because she was ashamed. She made me promise to wait and not tell anyone until after her divorce became final and we were married."

"Divorce?" Maisie was shocked. "Our faith does not allow divorce, Gavin. Annie might have remarried but Nathan never would have been able to. She knew that."

"She never filed for her divorce," Gavin said.

"Why not?" Nathan's words were as brittle as glass.

"She learned she was pregnant. She couldn't come to terms with having left you and taken your child away, too. If we had married the child would have been legally mine, and before you ask, yes, they are yours, Nathan, and not just because you were still her legal husband when they were born."

Nathan looked at Maisie and gave her a half smile. "It would make no difference. They are part of my heart and soul now."

Gavin shoved his hands in his pockets. "I tried to make her happy, tried to find a way to keep her with me, but I could feel her slipping away. I know she loved me and my children, but her guilt eventually drove a wedge between us. Finally, she told me she was going back to you. I didn't want to lose her, but I wanted her to find peace, so I let her go. I should have been with her."

"I'm sorry for your loss," Nathan said, surprising Maisie.

A tear slipped down Gavin's cheek as he looked at Nathan. "Thank you. I came here to say goodbye to her, but also to ask for your forgiveness. We wronged you and I am so, so sorry."

Nathan held out his hand. "You have my forgiveness and so does she. There is no need to ask for it."

Gavin took Nathan's hand and nodded but didn't speak. Then he walked away.

Maisie picked up one basket and Nathan picked up the other. Together they walked down the hill as Gavin got in his car and drove away.

"At least we have some answers," she said as she paused at the door of the cabin. What was Nathan thinking? She was ashamed of her sister's actions, but love made people do foolish things.

"I'm glad to finally understand what made Annie leave me, but it doesn't change what I have to say to you." He gazed at her intently. "I'll put away the mare and then we'll talk."

She flushed and hurried inside. Once the babies were in their cradles, they relaxed and went to sleep. Buddy curled up in his usual place between them.

Maisie was anything but relaxed. She went into the kitchen and saw her apple pie sitting on the counter. Tears pricked the backs of her eyes, but she refused to let them fall. She was done crying over Nathan Weaver. She had her own life to live.

She crossed her arms and leaned against the counter, waiting for him to come in. It wasn't long before he walked through the door and hung up his hat.

"How much of my conversation with Gemma did you overhear?" she asked before he could say anything.

He walked slowly into the kitchen and leaned back on the counter beside her. "Enough, I think. I heard you tell Gemma that you loved me. Did you mean it?"

She tried to brazen it out. "What does it matter?"

"It matters more than you know. I never expected to hear you say those words."

"I never expected to feel that emotion. I tried not to."

"Why?"

She bit down on her lower lip until it stopped quivering. "Do you really have to ask?"

"If I'm going to get this right, I need an answer. We already know how badly I messed up when I tried this on my own."

"If you're going to make me say it, I didn't want to love you because I knew you would never feel the same toward me."

He ran a hand through his hair. "Yesterday I would've said that you were right."

"So there. It's out in the open. I don't want your pity."

"Of all the emotions running through my head right now I can promise you pity is not one of them," he said.

"Are we done? Because I'd like to go lie down for a little bit. I have a headache."

"And your headache's name is Nathan."

"Those are your words." She started to walk past him, but he took her arm. "Maisie, look at me."

She couldn't. She was afraid he would see how close she was to breaking down.

"Maisie, I want to marry you," he said softly.

She cringed inside. He had no idea how much he was hurting her. She longed to say yes but she knew it would only bring her heartache. "We've been over this."

"We have had this conversation but that was before."

"Before Gavin came?"

"Before you opened my eyes. I heard what you were afraid of when you were talking to Gemma. But you haven't heard what I'm afraid of."

She looked at him then. His face was grim. "I have been afraid since I was young that no one really wanted me. My father died when I was four. My mother died when I was ten. I went from home to home, never really being a part of the family. For one reason or another none of them could keep me. I thought it was my fault. I thought I was different. I believed it was better to be alone. Then I met Annie."

"I know you loved my sister."

"I surely did. Then just when I thought God had led me to the place where I finally belonged, she left. It did more than break my heart. It shattered my faith in God. Watching you care for the babies and for me over these last days gave me a glimmer of hope. My faith started mending. Maisie, I don't want to marry you for the sake of the babies or because it's the sensible thing to do. I want to marry you for my own sake. Because I love you and I don't want to live without you at my side."

Maisie could feel her resolve weakening but she couldn't let go of her doubts. He didn't mean it. He couldn't. "You love Annie. Every time you look at me, you see her. That's who you are in love with."

"I thought so, too, but I was so wrong. You once told me that you and Annie were twins but you weren't the same." He cupped her chin and lifted her face. "I see you, Maisie."

"You see her shadow."

"I don't. Maisie has flecks of gold in her green eyes." He leaned forward and kissed her eyelid. "Maisie has a freckle right here that Annie never had. Maisie has amazing faith. She has a wonderful and spectacular heart. The likes of which I have been searching for my whole life."

Maisie was afraid to believe what she was hearing. She couldn't speak for fear she would say something that would drive him away and she didn't want him to go.

"I haven't convinced you?" There was a smile in his voice.

"You haven't."

"Maisie has a temper."

"I'm working on overcoming that."

"Don't work too hard at it. I find I admire a woman who can give me a piece of her mind and argue with me and still make me want to kiss her."

Maisie pressed her lips tightly together. She wanted to be kissed but not because she looked like the woman he loved.

"Oh, Maisie, what can I say that will make you hear me and not your doubts? You see into my heart. You know what I'm feeling the way Annie never did. I see a hundred ways in which you are different from your sister and I love every one of them."

"You said you loved my sister, too. How can I be sure this love is for me and not something left from loving her?"

"I did fall in love with your sister. I will never tell you differently. As I have gotten to know you, I have grown to love you. I didn't *fall* in love with you. My love grew so slowly I didn't know it was happening. Then it was there, like a sunflower forever turning its face to the sun. You are the woman who loves my children as much as I do. A woman who has a strong and enduring faith in God. I love you, Maisie. Not because you look like Annie or because you cook for me and keep my house, but in spite of all that. More than anything, I trust you will always love me and never leave me."

"How can you be so sure?"

"Because I have seen what kind of woman you are. I see your love for me in the way your eyes light up when I walk into the room. I feel it when your hand touches mine. I hear it in your voice even when you're scolding me. It took me a while to figure it out, but I'm sure now. I love you, Maisie whatever-your-middle-name-is. I'm going to kiss you. Speak up if you have any objections."

It was all happening so fast. "I'm sure something will occur to me."

He smiled. "Until it does." He pulled her close and pressed his lips to hers.

Every doubt and worry she had fell away as her heart soared with happiness. She slipped her arms around his neck and returned his kiss with all the joy in her soul. She loved him and he loved her. She would never doubt it again. When he drew away, she reluctantly let him go.

He sighed and tucked her head beneath his chin. "Have I convinced you?"

"Not totally."

He chuckled. "I should've known. What will it take?"

"If you would hold me like this forever and never let me go I might be convinced."

"Oh, if only I could but the *kinder* will want to be fed soon. Will you marry me, Maisie?"

"I think I will have to." She leaned back to look up at him. "How else can I show you how much I love you?"

"You could start with another kiss?"

She cupped his face with her hands. "Far be it from me to argue about such an important issue."

He gave her a quick peck on the lips. "Is this how I win one of our squabbles?"

She pressed a finger to his lips. "*Nee*, but I suspect we will have fewer in the future."

He laughed and hugged her tightly. "I'm not so sure about that, my love."

"We should notify the bishop of our decision soon. He'll be surprised."

"Don't be too sure. It was his idea."

She pushed back to look at him. "What was?"

"He suggested to me, because his wife suggested to him, that I should marry you and give the children a mother instead of a nanny."

"Did he really?"

"I thought it was a preposterous idea."

"Oh, you did? Was that why you proposed?"

"Something tells me I'm slipping onto thin ice again. What's for supper?"

* * *

Maisie burst out laughing, as he hoped she would. He wasn't the least bit interested in eating. He wanted to kiss her again. Nothing she baked could come close to the sweet taste of her lips. He laid his forehead against hers. "*Gott* took us on a roundabout path to each other, didn't he?"

She reached up to brush a lock of his hair off his face. "Perhaps that was so we will never take each other for granted."

He captured her hand and kissed her palm. "How soon can we marry? I don't want to wait another day to call you my own."

"Since we have both been married before we won't need a big ceremony. Two weeks after he reads the banns I'm guessing. We can join the church here at the same time."

"Do you want a big wedding?" He would give her whatever her heart desired.

"I had that. I don't need it again. Just a few of our new friends and neighbors will be fine."

"Then let's go see the bishop in the morning." He wanted to go now, but he knew she wouldn't want to wake the babies and take them out again.

A knock at the door made her move away from him. "Whoever it is, they have terrible timing," he muttered as he crossed the room and opened the door.

Lilly Arnett stood on the porch. "Is Maisie here?"

He stepped aside. "She is. Come in."

Lilly was grinning from ear to ear as she made a beeline into the kitchen. "I have the best news. The man who was going to rent my property has changed his mind. It's yours if you want it, Maisie."

His love laid one finger alongside her lips. "Did you hear that, Nathan? I can have a place of my own. What a tough decision."

He frowned. She was teasing him, wasn't she? He caught the twinkle in her eyes and crossed to her side. "Shall I help you pack?"

She laughed. "*Danki*, Lilly, but I won't be needing a place."

Lilly's face fell. "Oh. I'm sorry to hear that."

"I'm going to marry a lumberjack with a nice cabin that needs only a few minor improvements."

Lilly grinned. "The cabin or the lumberjack?"

Nathan chuckled as he draped his arm over Maisie's shoulders. "She'll improve both."

"Congratulations," Lilly said, taking Maisie's

hand. "The two of you deserve every happiness."

"Can you do us a favor?" Maisie asked suddenly. "Could you stay with the babies for a little bit?"

"Oh, I'd love to."

"*Danki*, we won't be long." Maisie took his hand and pulled him toward the door.

He followed her outside, curious as to where she wanted to go. There was a full moon rising in the east, giving enough light to see by. She chose the path that led to Lilly's house. Where was she going?

When they reached the bridge, she stopped. The moon shone down, making the rippling brook sparkle with reflected light. The sound of the stream rushing over the rocks drowned out everything but the beating of his heart as she gazed at him in the moonlight.

She cupped his face with her hands. "The first time I saw this bridge I knew you had built it."

"How?"

"I just did. I thought then it would be a wonderful place to kiss the man I love."

He drew her close. "Shall we see if it is?"

She smiled and wrapped her arms around his neck. "I thought you would never ask."

"What did I do to deserve you?"

She rose on tiptoe and whispered in his ear, "Only *Gott* knows that. I'm just following the path he set my feet upon." Then she kissed him, and he knew his heart was truly home.

* * * * *

Dear Reader,

When I was growing up I used to wish I had a twin. What fun that would have been. I also wished for a sister but one never showed up.

During my years as an NICU nurse I cared for hundreds of twins, a few triplets and even sextuplets. *There* is another story.

The parents of twins faced the same hardships as other new parents but their trouble wasn't double as long as they were both committed to caring for each other as well as their babies.

It isn't only the Amish who step up to help new families. We *Englisch* do it, too. Grandparents, aunts, sisters, brothers—they all come forward to help. It warms the heart to see so much shared love when love seems to be absent in our current society. It isn't, I assure you. Babies will always bring out the best in people. I think that's why God made them. They test our hearts and comfort our souls.

I hope you enjoyed reading about Nathan and Maisie. There are more North Country Amish stories coming in the future. Stay tuned.

Love to all,

Patricia Davids

Get 4 FREE REWARDS!

We'll send you 2 FREE Books plus 2 FREE Mystery Gifts.

Harlequin Heartwarming Larger-Print books will connect you to uplifting stories where the bonds of friendship, family and community unite.

FREE
Value Over
$20

HARLEQUIN SELECTS COLLECTION

19 FREE BOOKS IN ALL!

From Robyn Carr to RaeAnne Thayne to Linda Lael Miller and Sherryl Woods we promise (actually, GUARANTEE!) each author in the Harlequin Selects collection has seen their name on the *New York Times* or *USA TODAY* bestseller lists!

COURTING HIS AMISH WIFE
by Emma Miller
When Levi Miller learns Eve Summy is about to be forced to marry her would-be attacker or risk being shunned, he marries her instead. Now husband and wife, but complete strangers, the two have to figure out how to live together in harmony...and maybe even find love along the way.

HER PATH TO REDEMPTION
by Patrice Lewis
Returning to the Amish community she left during her *rumspringa*, widowed mother Eliza Struder's determined to redeem the wild reputation of her youth. But one woman stands between her and acceptance into the church—the mother of the man she left behind. Can she convince the community—and Josiah Lapp—to give her a second chance?

THE COWGIRL'S SACRIFICE
Hearts of Oklahoma • by Tina Radcliffe
Needing time to heal after a rodeo injury, Kate Rainbolt heads to her family ranch to accept the foreman job her brothers offered her months ago. But the position's already been filled by her ex-boyfriend, Jess McNally. With Jess as her boss—and turning into something more—this wandering cowgirl might finally put down roots...

A FUTURE TO FIGHT FOR
Bliss, Texas • by Mindy Obenhaus
Single father Crockett Devereaux and widow Paisley Wainwright can't get through a church-committee meeting without arguing—and now they have to work together to turn a local castle into a museum and wedding venue. But first they must put their differences aside...and realize they make the perfect team.

THE MISSIONARY'S PURPOSE
Small Town Sisterhood • by Kat Brookes
Wounded and back home after a mission trip, Jake Landers never expected his estranged friend Addy Mitchell to offer help. She hurt him by keeping secrets, and he's not sure he can trust her. But when their friendship sparks into love, can he forgive her...and give her his heart?

FINDING HER COURAGE
by Christine Raymond
Inheriting part of a ranch is an answer to prayers for struggling widow Camille Bellamy and her little girl—except Ty Spencer was left the rest of it. They strike a bargain: he'll agree to sell the ranch if she helps plan an event that could keep his business afloat. But can their arrangement stay strictly professional?